Jimmy O'Connell was born in Dublin, has been writing and performing his work for many years in various venues. His poetry has appeared in 'The Baltimore Review', 'Poetry Ireland Review', 'Stepaway Magazine', 'Flare 7 & 10', 'Poetry for a New Ulster' and 'Lime Square Poets', Voices from the Land, New Worlds New Voices Anthology, among others. A collection of his poetry, 'Although it is Night', was published by Wordonthestreet in 2013. His first published novel was 'Batter the Heart'.

In memory of my parents
Richard and Patricia O'Connell

Jimmy O'Connell

DEATH IN GARRYDANGAN

AUSTIN MACAULEY PUBLISHERS™
LONDON • CAMBRIDGE • NEW YORK • SHARJAH

Copyright © Jimmy O'Connell 2023

The right of Jimmy O'Connell to be identified as author of this work has been asserted by the author in accordance with sections 77 and 78 of the Copyright, Designs and Patents Act 1988.

All rights reserved. No part of this publication may be reproduced, stored in a retrieval system, or transmitted in any form or by any means, electronic, mechanical, photocopying, recording, or otherwise, without the prior permission of the publishers.

Any person who commits any unauthorised act in relation to this publication may be liable to criminal prosecution and civil claims for damages.

This is a work of fiction. Names, characters, businesses, places, events, locales, and incidents are either the products of the author's imagination or used in a fictitious manner. Any resemblance to actual persons, living or dead, or actual events is purely coincidental.

A CIP catalogue record for this title is available from the British Library.

ISBN 9781398499713 (Paperback)
ISBN 9781398499720 (ePub e-book)

www.austinmacauley.com

First Published 2023
Austin Macauley Publishers Ltd®
1 Canada Square
Canary Wharf
London
E14 5AA

Thanks to my family, to Sean Ruane, Paul O'Leary, Clare O'Reilly for their support, insights and encouragement.

Also to the Mullingar Writers Group, 'Inklings', for the opportunity they offer to try out new writings and their critiques and encouragement.

Table of Contents

Prologue	11
Chapter 1	23
1954 Marian Year	
Chapter 2	30
Chapter 3	36
Chapter 4	49
Chapter 5	56
Chapter 6	63
Chapter 7	70
Chapter 8	79
Chapter 9	84
Chapter 10	92
Chapter 11	103
Chapter 12	109
Chapter 13	113
Chapter 14	122
Chapter 15	133
Chapter 16	143

Chapter 17	**146**
Chapter 18	**151**
Chapter 19	**154**
Chapter 20	**157**
Chapter 21	**169**
Chapter 22	**175**
Chapter 23	**184**
Chapter 24	**191**
Chapter 25	**194**
Chapter 26	**198**
Chapter 27	**204**
Epilogue	**211**

Prologue

Stanley Payten drove by Rathnashee quarry which was nestled within the Esker Rí hills south of Garrydangan. An old rusted Bedford lorry was parked by badly hung gates. Stanley wasn't sure if the quarry was still in use because the lorry looked weary and seemed to plead for retirement.

It was Sunday morning. He rounded a corner carefully, fearing that on this particular narrow Irish country road he would encounter an oncoming tractor or a car on its way to Mass in St Fiacha's Church.

To say that St Fiacha's was unprepossessing was an understatement. This was no neo-gothic, proud granite church, with statement-making bell tower that he had seen as he drove through Maynooth, Kinnegad and Clochdroode. This was a grey cruciform barn of low roof and mealy aspect, tucked into the unassuming Esker hills.

Despite this, it was a busy place. Mass goers were walking, singly, or as a family, cycling, or travelling by the few cars that were parked by the sparse gravelly ditch and dusty hedges. He was late, deliberately so. He was shy among these people and their baronies, fields and houses. It was a very different world from the journalist scene of London, and the bachelor flat in Dulwich he had left on the previous day.

A different world and a different people. But he had made his decision to come among them and he would follow through with his task.

Charles Branagan, his editor, had called him from his Evening Standard office.

"Like you to do a piece on Irish Catholicism post the Papal Visit."

"When was that?" Stanley had asked, not a little embarrassed at revealing his ignorance.

"Just over five years ago," Charles raised his voice in feigned shock, "looks like I know more about Ireland than you do."

Stanley hoped this did not prove a mark against him. He needed the assignment. The rent was due. He also knew that his editor was Catholic, old English Catholic. He had to be careful not to offend.

"I know you have Irish roots," Charles said to Stanley, "you'll have a bit of a feel for this one. This Polish pope is causing quite the stir."

Of course he didn't tell Charles that he had no interest whatsoever in Irish Catholicism, that he saw it, basically, as a dangerous superstition, and that the Polish pope while obviously charismatic was probably a charlatan like all the rest of them. His Irish mother wasn't religious, but she did insist on him attending Mass with her every Sunday. That lasted until he was about twelve, when Norris Bingley had challenged him to prove to him that it was scientifically possible for a Catholic priest to turn a piece of bread and a cup of wine into the body and blood of Jesus Christ. He then proceeded to equate the Catholic religion with cannibalism.

He had a point, Stanley recalled. He had never recovered from that scientific blow to his theological system, shaky as it was in any case.

"Of course, Charles. Love to get my teeth into that."

Charles advised that he make suitable and appropriate contacts with Irish intellectuals, commentators, clerics, and of course 'the ordinary pious folk'. He noted Charles', possibly unconscious, English derision for the Irish peasant class. Charles obviously came from the pre-Tudor branch of Catholic aristocrats, with an aristocrat's disdain for the lower orders.

As part of his research Stanley phoned his only Irish contact Denis 'Dinny' Costello who worked in The Irish Times. Dinny, as was his very Irish way, was more than happy to have him 'stay over' for as long as he wanted. Sure, he'd be only too delighted to link him in with the usual intelligentsia, religious and secular and, sure, there was 'no shortage of opportunity for *vox populi*, as much as was wanted'.

Dinny picked Stanley up at Dublin airport and brought him to his house in Sandymount, a fine Edwardian pile, with leaking pipes and an obvious need for a lick of paint. "Sure, we'll get to that when we have time," Dinny said as he introduced his wife Norah, who gave him a hug as if he were a lost son of the tribe.

Over thick slices of beef, baked potatoes, 'lashings of gravy', French beans and carrots, and with the aid of a nice red, rather expensive, Bordeaux (which Stanley had brought with him from Barretts Wine Merchants, Oxford Street), 'Ah, sure you shouldn't have', they discussed a range of subjects from the politics of print journalism, to national and international politics, and of course, 'The Troubles above in the North'.

As he sat in his car outside the parish church, Stanley recalled the conversation about the subject at hand, religion, Catholicism, and the impact or not, thereof, of the 1979 Papal Visit.

"Don't underestimate the anti-clericalism at the heart of the Irish people," Dinny said as he poured the third bottle from his store of Chianti (the Bordeaux had been binned hours earlier). "But, mind, never underestimate the power of the Church either."

"We saw that in the referendum," Norah was in and out of the kitchen carrying food-crusted plates, used knives and forks, as well as serving dishes of rhubarb tart, fresh whipped cream and thick slices of what they called 'sixpenny ice-creams', cut, or hacked, from a block of HB raspberry ripple ice-cream.

"The referendum?"

"Do ye Brits not follow Irish goings on at all, at all," Dinny jested. "The abortion referendum."

"Of course," Stanley lifted his wineglass as excuse, "sure ye have me moidered with the drink."

"Good man," Dinny raised his glass, "a fine and much used term used to excuse all bad behaviour, and all and sundry."

Norah was particularly exercised and annoyed at the outcome of the referendum. "It's now unconstitutional to seek or have an abortion here in Ireland."

"Won't make a whit of difference," Dinny said, "women will find ways."

"Yes. The boat to Liverpool. And sure, when the poor girl returns the family will tell the neighbours, 'Sure she was away in England visiting her sister.'" Adding with derision, "Me eye."

What he learned, at least from a Sandymount-Donnybrook, liberal point of view, was that the Papal Visit was both a success and a last gasp. As Dinny explained, "However, from the people's point of view (Did he mean the ordinary folk? He did not elaborate), it was an historic and important occasion."

From what the Costellos were saying, Stanley got the impression that the Mass in the Phoenix Park, which attracted nearly a million people, was more or less a promotional success. It was presided over by a 'singing Bishop and a trendy Priest', the music was 'fantastic', the pomp and ceremony was a 'theatrical success', but that it was full of 'gawkers' and not the 'sincere' Catholics.

"Gawkers?" Stanley asked.

"Gawkers, you know, kids who were out for a good day, a bit of craic. Sure even Stephen (their son) went with a group from UCD. Sure we thought he got religion, or something. But he enjoyed it; said he found it interesting."

"Drogheda did it for me," Norah said.

She sat at the table, some dishes still to be cleared, but she wanted to make a particular point.

"Drogheda was where the Pope was to speak out against the IRA. That's okay. I hoped he would. And he did. In his way. Appealed to their better natures to give up violence. I had some hope that he would be listened to. After all, they are bloody Catholics, even if they are Nationalists and Republicans. But they slapped him in the face. There was no change. They went on with their bombings and murdering, as if he never said a word. That's what did it for me. I knew then the Church was gone. It had no power. It had thrown their last dice, placed its reputation and power and influence on achieving something real, tangible and lasting. And it failed. Miserably."

"Ireland doesn't have a Catholic Church, Stanley," Dinny poured more wine into his half empty glass, "not anymore. I mean in the sense that it has any influence in a religious or spiritual sense. It used to have. But now it is a hollow of a husk of an empty promise. It promises but can never deliver."

This conversation was not what Stanley expected. He obviously had an out-dated version of Irish Catholicism. Would his mother have recognised it? Probably not.

It was near to midnight when Norah noted Stanley flagging with tiredness said, "For Gods sakes Dinny, let the man go to bed. He has a long day ahead of him tomorrow."

It was now fifteen minutes into the Mass. Stanley was hesitant to go into the church. Should he just wait until the people had left and then go in? But he felt drawn into it. And anyway it would give a flavour as to how the Irish did it. He culled from memory his First Holy Communion and the Sunday Masses he had attended, the Catholic funerals and weddings, not his own. From what he remembered, the Mass usually started on the hour and there were readings, a sermon and then the central, main part, the Communion.

He got out of the car. It was chilly. The sky charcoal with coming rain. Luckily, he had brought an anorak. He put it on. The air was heavy with the smell of cattle, dung and diesel; the autumn fields displaying proud farming activity. He had to go through an ancient wrought iron rusted gate. It creaked as he swung it open. It closed itself with a strain. The main door was open. Some men were standing half-in half-out. They were mostly middle-aged and elderly, wearing heavy woollen coats, worn and bare-threaded. Coats taken out of the wardrobe only on a Sunday, he imagined, hanging there maybe for decades, maybe even passed on down from father or uncle to son or nephew. One man knelt on one knee on his flat cap with a rosary in his angular farmer's hands, his left hand holding his forehead reverently while his right hand moved the beads one at a time through his fingers, his nails black with farm dirt.

The men looked at him as he made his way through them, neither welcoming nor preventing. They nodded to him, indicating that if he wanted to go inside they would move for him. He did, curiosity getting the better of shyness and a reluctance to be in the way of their weekly prayers.

Inside was tiny. He was shocked at how close he was to the altar and was almost overwhelmed by the stale smell of sweat and the clinging wet of late autumn. He thought he might be able to protect his anonymity, but when he moved past the door and into the short, narrow nave he suddenly became the centre of attention. He almost turned to walk out, but the attention was momentary and though there was interest and fascination in his presence, it lasted but the length of a side-glance, or a brief nod of inquisitiveness. A strange sense of not being odd came over him. He felt as if they were treating him as one of them. Though he was a stranger, it unnerved him to feel that, in fact, he could have been one of them, as if he were someone who had just arrived late to Mass due to the car failing to start, or a sick animal delayed him. It shocked him, to the point of disorientation. A quiet tremulousness sighed through his body, as if he were, at last, discovering the right and apposite pitch commensurate with this particular moment.

His eyes caught the side-glance of a young woman. She was in her twenties. She was pretty, had an intelligent face, green-blue eyes, a beautifully sculpted forehead, cheek and chin. Her auburn hair was covered by a fashionable silk scarf. His mind stimulated to recognition. Did he know this young woman? She seemed so familiar. He looked again. He never saw her in his life, but he could not shake the feeling of familiarity. She could have been his mother when she lived here decades ago. He cast his eyes over others in the tiny chapel. Again, there was that uncanny commonality. The men young and old, the women, children, each and every one could have been someone he knew from somewhere in the past, and maybe not even his own past, maybe from his tribal past. He knelt down on one knee beside one of one old man who shuffled to one side to make room for him.

A piercing clattering sound echoed through the tiny church. It was a set of bells being shook almost with glee by a young altar boy dressed in a black soutane and white lace-frilled surplice. It drew his attention to the priest. He was an old man, ascetic, angular, with thin grey hair. He was bent over a gold chalice but was holding a large white host in his two hands. Stanley was mesmerised by his movements.

The priest bowed, inclined his head as if he were in conversation with it. Then frowned at the host, nodded and frowned again, and, in a slow, deep, clear voice, intoned with the utmost reverence, "This…" He then paused, nodded three times, frowned and repeated, in a whisper, "This…" and then shouted, "This is my…" He paused, "This is my…" He paused again, "Body!" The word bellowed out in a tenor voice which filled the small crowded spaces, and with deep reverence he lifted the host.

Stanley looked around to see how the congregation was responding. It disturbed him. He hadn't seen or heard this before. But they didn't seem to be perturbed. Maybe it was normal, but he suspected that this old priest was either senile or there was something amiss.

The altar boy's eyes were glued to the priest. He shook the bells for as long as the priest held up the host displaying it to the congregation.

He must have held it up for at least ten seconds. Maybe that was an exaggeration but to Stanley there was something very odd here. He looked at the young woman. She had her head bowed in reverence and did not seem to think this was unusual.

The priest placed the host on the altar, genuflected, took the chalice in his hands, and again seemed to be speaking to it. He nodded, again three times, bowed his head and repeated as before, "This." Pause. "This is my…"

He lifted the chalice over his head, presenting it to the congregation, and shouted, "Blood!" And repeated, louder, "Blood!"

And again, his voice filled the tightly packed space.

During the distribution of Communion Stanley decided to return to his car and wait. A slight drizzle fell from a thick grey sky. The wind flung it onto the windscreen in irregular sweeps, blurring Stanley's vision of the tiny church.

When he got the assignment to write about the post-Papal Visit Ireland, he obviously thought of Garrydangan. It had been his mother's parish. He came here for research, but that wasn't the only, or real, reason. He had asked Dinny Costello to find out if there was a current list of priests in each parish available. Dinny told him he was sure The Irish Times would have records that they keep updated. His mother told him that Father Daniel O'Byrne was the name of her priest at the time she left for England. Was this the same Father O'Byrne his mother spoke of? Did Dinny manage to find the same person? Was he the one to speak to? Maybe it was a mistake. Dinny told him that there was a priest with the same name in Rathnashee, but it wasn't far from Garrydangan, it might be the same man. There must be hundreds of priests with the same name all over Ireland. But somehow he knew this was the same man.

What would he gain from a priest who behaved so oddly, even so disturbingly? Any time he had attended Mass, as far as he could recall, the priest was calm, spoke in quiet reverend tones, and moved around the altar with a kind of holy dignity. But this priest was different. Yet the congregation did not seem to be upset or embarrassed for him. This seemed to them to be normal behaviour. But surely it wasn't.

There was almost a King Lear aspect to him. If he had seen this man in a theatrical production of Lear, the chilling madness of the King would have been palpable. The awful conversation with the host and chalice was like the insane King on the mad moors. And yet there was no reaction from the people. Maybe it was accepted by them as an act, a religious-theatrical event, that took place every Sunday to which they returned over and over again. All part of the normal weekly ritual.

He sat in the car until he was sure the congregation had left. He watched the pretty young woman get on her bicycle and cycle away, probably back to her family, either as wife and mother, sister or daughter. He tried to catch her eye as she passed, to nod to her, maybe get into conversation and interview her about her experience of the Pope's visit, she would make a good interviewee, he was sure. But that wasn't why he was here. The article was on hold for the moment. It could wait.

He hadn't seen the priest leave so he assumed he was still in the church. When he thought everyone had left, when all the bicycles had gone and the last car driven past, he decided to go in and meet him.

He walked up the aisle of the empty chapel. The musty smells of damp walls and the bodies of the congregation hung like an invisible fog as he made his way towards the sanctuary area. Stanley sighed with disappointment. The priest had gone. But he heard a noise, it seemed to be metallic. It came from a small room to the right of the altar. Stanley walked into the sanctuary and looked into the sacristy. The old priest was alone, bending down to pick up the chalice he had let slip from his hand. As he turned to see who had entered, Stanley noticed the painfully stiff movements of the old priest. His face was lined with suffering; his eyes strained with some deep anxiety and fear. He looked at Stanley, turned away from him, seemed to pretend that he wasn't there. It was obvious he didn't want to be disturbed.

"Father O'Byrne?" Stanley addressed the old man as he quietly and slowly entered.

"Who are you?" the priest asked gruffly, turning his bent back to him.

"Stanley Payten."

"Who?" The priest turned to take another look at the visitor. He frowned with annoyance at this disturbance, "Never heard of you."

"You knew my mother."

"What? What are you saying?"

"She's from, or was from, Garrydangan."

"How the hell would I know your mother?"

"Her name was Anne. Anne Connaughton."

The old priest slumped onto the floor. "Oh, God." His voice now raspy and pained, "No!"

Chapter 1
1954 Marian Year

"Ah, for God's sakes, John, ya have to do something about this."

Frank Dalton screamed at John Holton, team manager, local Garda, and who was also secretary of St Michael's GAA club. John had a good mind to turn to his friend and tell him to shut up and leave him alone, but he couldn't do it in public, not that he could do it in private either. Dalton was not the kind of man who would take any correction, or any public challenge to his person.

It was Pattern Day, celebrating the local Patron Saint, Fiacha, and what was taking place, and which was exercising the wrath of at least one parent, was the annual under 16s Pattern Match between Saint Michael's parish which included Garrydangan and Clochdroode, and their rivals, Fanmore.

The match was played on a bright and unusually warm summer's day, which had attracted a larger than usual number of spectators. Even Father Dan O'Byrne, the local curate, was in attendance. A young jowly man with thick black wiry hair and a pre-mature paunch. He had agreed to attend because, after all, it was Pattern Day in the Marian Year and he himself had been central in organising this special Pattern Day. A

High Mass was concelebrated in St Michael's Church with the parish priest, Father Leo Caffery, earlier in the morning, and before the throw-in he had gathered his parishioners together, in the middle of the football pitch, to say the Glorious Mysteries of the Rosary; and on the following day, Sunday, there would be a Mass with the local choir singing Panis Angelicus, and later, at seven o'clock, to end Pattern weekend, Benediction.

Local families came out to support their sons' team. The Keane's, the Ruanes, the MacDonaghs, the Eagans, Geoghans and Dalys; and while most of the spectators were men, there were many women with children who came out to play among themselves, enjoy the sun and have a picnic. The mothers of the players prepared plates of ham sandwiches, cake and red lemonade which would be consumed by both sides after the football match.

A huge shout of joy and loud clapping could be heard from the far side of the football pitch as Fanmore scored yet another point. Fanmore were now ahead by four points.

"Take off that Keane lad, John, he hasn't a clue." Dalton shouted at John Holton, "Sure, he's been made a fool of out there. Put Frankie into the forwards and he'll score for us."

Tomás Keane, the father of young Keane referred to, stood on the sideline, within earshot. He scowled at Frank Dalton, who was only interested in making sure his son, Frankie, became the hero of the day, but said nothing. He had to be careful not to stir up trouble. Sylvia, his wife, had warned him not to be shouting at Michael, and telling him what to do and who to mark. "Sure, if you want to be manager then go ahead," she told him. "But you know as well as anyone that that's never going to happen."

A groan went out from the St Michael's side as Frankie Dalton went on a long solo-run from the backs, and with teammates on either side, one of them Michael Keane, screaming at him for a pass, took aim from about forty yards out and kicked the ball twenty feet wide.

"What are ye at, ya fecken loodermawn!" Tomás Keane screamed in a blind moment of apoplexy. "Why didn't ye pass it to Michael?"

Frankie Dalton, a big lad, almost adult in size, with a square head and sandy hair, ran back to his position turned towards where he heard the criticism and shouted, "Ah, fuck off with yerself!"

"That's it, Frankie, you tell him," his father shouted as he turned to Keane.

Someone, it was either Seamus Heneghan or Vinnie Tarpey, mumbled quietly to Tomás, "Never mind him, he's only an old bollix, we can still win this."

Tim Dooley, the sacristan, was smiling to himself as he stood just behind Father O'Byrne. He could see Father O'Byrne's growing agitation.

"Ah, come on, lads, watch the language," could be heard along the line, "the priest is watching."

Dalton turned to the priest, raised his hand in acknowledgement, and mumbled a reluctant apology.

A cheer went up as Michael Keane caught a high ball in centre field and soloed up field. Frankie Dalton was running just ahead of him, screaming for a pass. Michael dodged and beat a defender and laid off a quick pass to him. A huge cheer of anticipation went up as Frankie caught the ball and was making his way towards the Fanmore goal.

"That's it, lad," his father shouted encouragement, "put it over the bar."

Michael Keane ran forward calling to Frankie expecting a return pass.

John Holton, shouted at Frankie, "Give it to Michael. Pass the fecken ball to Michael."

But it was ignored. Frankie's father shouted, "That's it, go on, lad, go on for the point."

Frankie thundered forward like a young bull towards the goal. He kicked the ball but scuffed it. The ball bounced away from him and rolled harmlessly into the hands of a Fanmore defender, who kicked it back into the St Michael's goal area. A huge cheer was heard from both sides of the field; the mothers and children who weren't, up to this moment, paying attention, lifted their heads in the direction of the cheers.

There was a scramble for the ball, and in a twinkle of an eye, without anyone realising how it happened, the ball was in the back of the St Michael's net.

A torrent of abuse went up on the St Michael's side.

Men were screaming at one another:

"Who the fuck picked this shaggin' team?"

"What in the name of God was the goalie doing?"

"Ah, ref, are ye blind, he threw the fuckin' ball into the net. Ya can't do that!"

With only a few minutes to go, Fanmore were now ahead by seven points. The men on St Michael's side of the field grew more and more angry at what was happening, or not happening, on the field of play.

Fanmore seemed to be always first to the ball, and St Michal's either fluffed a catch, a pickup, or were marking too loosely. Each time a player from Michael's made a mistake, some father shouted abuse to either their own son, or someone else's.

The atmosphere was becoming intense with anger, anxiety and recrimination. The women and children, who were largely uninterested with what was going on, became uneasy and sensed a coming storm of abuse, started to gather their children into prams, and to the children who were crying because they didn't want to leave, told them that they had to go home to get the tea ready.

At last, the referee blew the final whistle and the Fanmore team and supporters ran onto the field, embraced one another and shook one another's hands. On the St Michael's side, there was shouting, and fists raised. Someone, maybe it was Dalton, or it could have been one of the Egan's or the Daly's shouted, "Fucken useless blow-ins' and 'bloody migrants'."

Others could be heard swearing, "What's that you said?" To which was answered, "You fucken heard me, ya migrant. Go back to where ye came from."

Father O'Byrne found himself caught in the middle, and was jostled about as men who, screaming abuse at one another in their anger and unchecked violence, were mindless of the presence of their priest.

Tim Dooley moved in beside Father O'Byrne, held him firmly by the elbow and tugged him back in the direction of the gate, "Come on, Father, we'd better leave."

Father O'Byrne was too shocked to resist. By the time he got to his car, he had sufficiently recovered his senses and was about to turn and make his way back to the melee that was unfolding on the football pitch. "I have to go back and tell them to behave themselves."

Tim, who had not let go of the priest, said, "You'd better get into your car, Father. This will sort itself out in time."

"I have to go back in there and stop this savagery."

Tim Dooley managed to convince Father O'Byrne to return to the parish house. He wondered, as he watched the black Morris Minor turn and drive back to Garrydangan, how much the priest knew about the history of his parish, or if he did, to what extent was he, or should be, surprised at the anger and resentment that lay just below the surface of a seeming quiet country parish.

He walked back towards the football pitch. He could see John Holton, the local Garda, raising and waving both hands to the crowd of men. He may have been acting in his role of Guardian of the Peace but was not very effective. Other men were helping him by separating what seemed to be two factions, and telling them to calm the fuck down, "Sure, it's only a game. Come on, lads, let's give over this."

Tim, as with every parishioner, knew who the factions were. He could name them. It had nothing to do with football, or the GAA, or even the young lads on the pitch. There were two factions, the 'blow-ins', or 'migrants', and the 'locals'. The Mayo 'migrants' who 'took' Land Commission farms, and locals who resented them taking what they believed 'belonged' to them. Of course, it never belonged to them, but to the 'big' Landlords who lived either in England or in the local Big Houses, or on Dublin's Merrion Square.

Tim stood at the gate and watched what was happening. A spectator at a melee. He took out his packet of Sweet Aftons, tapped a cigarette on the box, and lit it. He shook his head and smiled, "God help us all. Sure, will they never get it into their heads that there's not a chance of us ever winning a bloody All-Ireland unless 'migrants' play for us. And Jays, God only knows when that will happen."

Chapter 2

Frankie Dalton waited until the summer light dimmed in the west and the greying night seeped its way into Garrydangan, to put Dodger, his mixed terrier, on a leash and lead him out by the Droode River. He'd take the route by the Old Mill. That'd mean he'd be able to sneak in without being seen.

In the darkening sky, the outline of the mill, its bleak ruined stone walls, loomed over him as Dodger pulled him forward, eager to be where his master was taking him. Frankie Dalton was a big lad for his age, almost six foot in height, he had the gait and amble of a boxer. And, like a boxer, seemed always ready to pounce and jab. At first glance, one would think he was handsome with well-set chin and deep forehead, but on closer inspection one noticed his cheeks were wider than what was considered in proportion, and his eyes, though blue, did not sparkle with intelligence. If one were to look into his eyes, as he passed the ghost like shapes of the now redundant water wheel and the empty skeleton windows towering over him, one would see fear created by a mind too easily affected by the conjuring of such gothic images. But once he passed by it, his breathing eased and he let out a loud relieving yelp at the blackening clouds above.

He walked by the demesne wall of Tyrrell House, found the gap he was looking for which would lead out by the old quarry. Once there all he had to do was walk the old sheep track which led to the back of the Keane and Heneghan farms which were adjacent to one another.

During Mass last Sunday Frankie sat with his father, while his mother sat with the women on the other side of the aisle. Father O'Byrne was giving out to the congregation from the pulpit. He heard the priest saying things about the disgraceful behaviours during the football match. "And it the feast of our own, our very own saint, Fiacha, a man of God," he shouted at them. Frankie didn't see how it was a disgrace. And then the priest went on about letting down God and disobeying the law of God. But Frankie wasn't paying much attention, he was trying to get a glimpse of the girls on the other aisle, turning his head sideways putting his hands on his forehead as if in deep thought but slyly glancing at their legs. Doreen Heneghan's legs were covered by a long coat. That was no fecken good. But Miss Connaughton's were by far the best. She wore a skirt that went just below the knee; she wore nylons, and he could see that her clothes were better than Doreen Heneghan's. They were more modern looking, like you'd see at the pictures.

The priest was still going on about the fight on Saturday and asking what he, as their priest, was to do with them all. Sure, what was he going to do? What could he do? Frankie became excited remembering how he got a hold of Michael Keane's head after the match, put it in a headlock the way he saw in the cowboy films, and hit him square in the face. The thrill of remembering it flowed through him to the extent that he wished he could start a fight with the Keanes after Mass and get them all into headlocks and beat the shite out of the whole lot of them.

And then when they got home his father and mother were giving out yards about the Priest's sermon. 'How dare he accuse us of letting ourselves down!' his mother said to his father as she opened the grocery section to sell the Sunday papers, sliced pans and cakes to the after-Mass crowd.

His father was putting on his brown working coat and checking that he had enough change in the till and muttering, "Bloody well come in here and think they own the place. As if they had more rights than them that's been living here for generations."

Frankie didn't really understand what his father meant by that. He carried out his usual Sunday morning chores, emptying boxes of beans, peas, sweets and cigarettes; sweeping the floor behind the counter, and opened the shop door when all was ready. Throughout the chores all he thought of was how he had tried to impress his father by scoring goals and points. His father never took heed of him only when he played football. It never occurred to Frankie to pass the ball to anyone else. Why should he? He had the ball in his hand, his father was shouting at him to score. If he had scored, his father would have told him what a great lad he was and that he'd be picked, surely, for the county. But he messed up and the memory of it cut like as if he had been gored by a hayfork. It was a relief to punch his way through the five or six men who were attacking him. It was no disgrace. He saw Tomás Keane grab his father by the lapel of his jacket and pull at him, trying to drag him away from one of the Tarpeys. Frankie with pure passion and love wanted to be the one to rescue his father and show him what a man he really was, but John Holton had separated them by the time he got there. He clenched his fist and punched a tree as he passed. "I'll get them. I'll get them," he kept saying as he made his way home.

He lay low by the ditch of the back field of the Keane farm. Dodger was growling with gleeful eagerness. He wanted more than anything to get at the sheep that were nibbling at the grass close by, unawares of the danger they were in. Frankie pulled on the chain lead, "Heel, Dodger, heel."

Frankie checked to see that no one had seen them. The silence of the summer evening was disturbed only by the breeze swishing the sycamore trees above and the barley in the next field. Heneghan's. He knew that as long as he remained on this side of the low hill he could not be seen. Keane's dog was barking, but Frankie wasn't concerned. It was always tied up at night, and anyway even if he did get loose, Dodger would be well able for him.

Dodger pulled on the leash and with snorting noises was eager to get at the sheep. Frankie pointed Dodger in the direction of one particular sheep. Frankie let him go, "Gwan, boy, gwan."

Dodger attacked the sheep and bit onto its neck and was about to bring it to the ground when the sheep pulled free. Dodger let out a yelp of disappointment, looked back at Frankie, to see what he would do. Frankie let out a command, "Go, boy, go on, git 'em."

The dog swerved around with delight and swooped on another sheep that was standing alone, as if paralysed. It grabbed the sheep by the neck and this time, like a wrestler, brought it down.

Frankie was delirious with joy at the way Dodger managed to pin the sheep to the ground.

"Attaboy. Attaboy."

He was so excited his mind was overwhelmed with both joy and intoxicating fear. He ran at the sheep, pulled out his knife and leaped onto the woolly creature, stabbing it over and over. The sight of blood flowing from the sheep's helpless body, and Dodger barking and tearing at the hind leg, drove Frankie into an ecstasy. He had never experienced anything so thrilling in his life before. This was exactly the feeling he had wanted when he scored a goal. But he had failed. But this more than made up for that disappointment. He stood up and looked down at the sheep and watched it as its breathing became shallower and shallower until, finally, there was no movement.

Frankie kicked the sheep to see if there was life. It didn't move, its woolly body grey and darkening.

He kicked at it again, and again. "Ha, attaboy," he screamed in delirious delight, "attaboy."

He could feel his body tensing. It was as if it were fusing with outside, unimagined dangers that created the excitement. His sense of hearing had sharpened. He could hear Keane's dog barking a warning, saw a band of light in the night sky.

"Here, boy, here, Dodger."

Dodger was about to chase another sheep, but the clear sharp command of his master made him turn and follow him over the ditch and back the way they had come.

Frankie washed his bloody hands in the Droode river by the mill and cleaned his knife. He put Dodger back on the leash and made his way back to his father's shop.

Frankie could hardly sleep with the excitement. He relived each stupendous and all-absorbing moment from the hiding in the ditch to the leaping forward like an ancient, tribal hunter, and the frenzied stabbing and the acrid smell of blood. He lay on his bed, giving thanks for what he had seen and done, the strength of his young body, the speed of his hands and his ability to think and plan, and, now, finally, in the dead of night, the moment of ease and satiation.

Two days later, Frankie awoke and, as usual, went out to feed Dodger and bring him for a walk. But he wasn't there. His kennel was empty. He went outside to see if he was waiting for him. Still no sign of him. Then from the corner of his eye he saw something moving in the tree by the shop. Dodger was hanging by a rope, his throat slit and dried blood staining his flawless dun coat.

Chapter 3

Anne Connaughton walked past the post office on her way to school.

Joey McDonagh, whom she taught, crossed the street, running to her with excitement. Miss Connaughton was a nice teacher and easy to talk to, "Miss, Miss."

"Good morning, Joey."

"Miss, did you hear?"

Anne Connaughton had heard but asked, "Heard what, Joey?"

"Jamesie says he saw a dog hanging from a tree yesterday."

Most of Garrydangan must have seen it, Anne thought. She hadn't seen it, but Josie Fagan, the post-mistress, was telling everyone who came to buy stamps or get their pension books stamped that she had seen it.

"There it was hanging outside Daltons. Shocking I tell you, shocking to the world. What's happening in a nice quiet village like this?"

Joey saw Maisie Egan, who was in his class and ran over to her telling her the exciting news.

As Anne walked into the yard the children were in groups whispering and laughing or whispering and shocked at what they had seen or heard. Anne determined that it was better not to say anything to her class about what happened, but knew it was going to be difficult to avoid the subject.

"Miss Connaughton," it was the principal, Louise O'Malley, standing at the entrance door her arms folded, "a moment, if you please."

Louise O'Malley was in her early forties and was, what Anne would describe as 'severe'. She was a handsome woman, tall and imperious. She seemed to feel that severity of mien, including a conservative choice of clothes, was what was expected of a principal of a primary school. This extended to her relationship with her junior teacher. Although Anne had been teaching in Garrydangan for the last four years, they never addressed one another other than by their titles and surnames. Miss O'Malley never asked personal questions of Anne, and in turn Anne never asked of her. It was mutually understood that there was a separation between personal and professional life. This suited Anne, although she would have welcomed some warmth and a more personable relationship with someone she worked with so closely. But, she had a job, as her mother reminded her, 'and as long as she treats you fairly and you get your wages, in the name of God, what else do you want?'

"Morning, Miss O'Malley," Anne was determined to be polite, "lovely day to day."

The principal looked at her, as if to say, there's more to be talked about than the weather.

Miss O'Malley was keeping a watchful eye on the children in the yard, it was important that they know that she had her eye on each and every one of them at all times, "I suppose, Miss Connaughton, you've heard what has happened."

"Yes, I heard people talking about it yesterday evening."

"Disgraceful behaviour. I have never heard of anything so bad in all my time here." She turned to look at Anne, expecting nothing else but complete cooperation, "If asked, Miss Connaughton, we tell the children that bad men came down from Dublin and did this."

Anne was about to say that it was ridiculous to pretend what everyone knew already.

"I won't have this school being sucked into some local bickering. Are we in agreement, Miss Connaughton?"

"Of course, Miss O'Malley, I understand."

"Remember, everything as normal, Miss Connaughton."

There was about five minutes to go before Michael Delamere from Sixth Class rang the bell for school to begin. Anne went into her classroom to check that everything was in order, and then, at the ringing of the bell, she went out to the yard and made sure her class was properly lined up, and then walked them into the classroom.

She said Morning Prayers, took the morning roll, and when they had settled into their desks she took out the Times Tables from the cupboard. She noticed an unease in the room. The incident at the football match on Pattern Day and now this business about Keane's sheep and the Dalton dog was beginning to affect her children. But these local tensions had been going on for a while now, she reminded herself. She recalled her first year in the school, almost four years ago. The children playing in the yard reminded her of her first encounter with Frankie Dalton.

It was during lunch break when it was her turn to supervise the yard. Some girls from Fifth and Sixth had come over to her to have a chat. Although she wasn't their teacher, the girls found her easy to talk to. They talked about clothes, what pictures they had gone to and of course, boys. There was commotion at the other end of the yard. A group of boys, mostly the older ones, were cheering and laughing. It was easy to see that it was no fun that was going on. Frankie Dalton was punching young Richard Kneafsey in the face and pushing him up against the wall. Anne immediately ran down to the group shouting at them to stop. Most of the boys turned at her warning and either ran or walked away, leaving Frankie and the Kneafsey lad still fighting one another, or rather as Anne realised when she came upon them, Richard Kneafsey was a lot smaller and younger than Frankie Dalton, and was getting the worst of the exchange.

Without thinking and without any hesitation she told Frankie to leave Richard alone, but he didn't. He defied her and continued to hit Richard in the stomach. Anne saw blood spilling for his nose. She grabbed Frankie by the arm and pulled at him ordering him to stop, but even then he was a big lad, almost fully grown. She had to pull at his arm again, this time getting her body between herself and young Kneafsey. It was still a struggle. Kneafsey slumped to the ground while Frankie was determined to beat him up.

Anne had no other choice but to get herself in front of Frankie and order him to go to the principal. He refused. Even now, Anne remembered the savagery of the look in his face, and the eyes that clearly told her how much he was enjoying beating this child. And she remembered clearly what she did next. She slapped him in the face with all the force she could muster. He was so shocked he stopped completely what he was doing. Suddenly he started to cry, and the tears flowed, and within a mere few seconds he was bawling with frustration. By then Miss O'Malley had come and told him to go straight home, that she would be talking to his mother. With that, he turned, looked at Anne with such hate she had never seen or felt in her life before. He walked away in the direction of his father's shop.

Anne thought that that would be end of it, that the principal would tell the Dalton parents to come in to see her and for Frankie Dalton to explain his behaviour. But nothing happened. At that time Anne was in no position to challenge the authority of her principal. After all, it was her first year. She couldn't contradict or tell the principal of the school what she ought to do. But it was the aftermath that was the most unsettling and almost cost her job.

Before the end of the school day, Mrs Dalton came to the school. But she hadn't come in to he told off by the principal for the misbehaviour and the bullying of a younger pupil by her son. Instead, she demanded that Anne be dismissed for hitting her child.

It was Anne who was called into the principal's classroom with Mrs Dalton present and asked to explain her behaviour. Anne could not believe what was happening. It soon became obvious that she was being treated as the guilty party. What was even more galling was the fact, or at least, the distinct impression, that Louise O'Malley agreed with the mother, or was intimidated by her. But Anne wasn't going to weaken, or cave in.

It was she who saw what Frankie did to young Richard Kneafsey. It was she who saw the blood, the terror in the poor child's eyes. It was she who remembered the girls from Sixth and Fifth complaining that Frankie was a bully and that he was always picking on kids younger than him. Anne told Mrs Dalton and the principal that she had asked the girls what had happened on that particular day. They told her that the lads told them that Frankie had been taunting Richie all morning calling him names, like 'Kneesie' and pushing him around the yard looking for a fight. 'Come on ya Mayo coward, come on and prove yer a man'.

It was Anne who saw those mad eyes, that crazy face, although she never used the terms 'mad' or 'crazy' in front of the two women. But she did tell them that she had no alternative but to slap him as you would someone who was in hysterics. "I had to do that in order to get his attention, to calm down."

She told her version of events in an objective and as dispassionate a manner as she could muster, but at the same time she was nervous and fearful of being sacked.

"But you hit my child, Miss Connaughton."

"I had to, Mrs Dalton," she appealed to Miss O'Malley for support, but wasn't confident that she was getting any. "I had to or he would have killed the child."

"Next thing you'll be accusing my child of murder. How dare you, Miss Connaughton. I'm going to Father O'Byrne about this."

And at that she left.

Anne was left standing with the principal alone in the room. She was told by the principal that the Manager of the school, Father O'Byrne, would be looking into the incident. And that was the end of the conversation.

The following day Anne was told by the principal to go to the priest's house after school. She knocked on the door and it was answered by Moll Daly, the housekeeper. She was shown into the parlour. It was furnished in the Victorian style, mahogany tables, dresser, straight-backed chairs and a painting of the Holy Family on the back wall. The curtains were of that heavy velvet type that seemed to be in all of the more important houses of the time.

Anne sat in the chair indicated which was adjacent to the window. She remembered it being a windy day and the hedge outside ruffled and the copper beech seemed to heave. She also recalled that it was the first time in her life that she had ever spoken to a priest face to face outside the confessional or a church.

Father O'Byrne entered, greeted her politely and took a seat opposite. Without any informalities she was asked simply to tell him what happened. She repeated more or less verbatim what she had told Mrs Dalton and the principal. He didn't take any notes. At the time Anne did not remark on it or consider it an issue. It was only later that she thought it odd and probably unprofessional and even more, possibly unjust. But, at that time, she was in no position to question or make a complaint.

When Anne had finished her narrative, she stopped and waited for him to speak. He looked out the window.

He was avoiding her eyes. She felt uncomfortable, but this had more to do with her own uncertainty as to how to behave with a priest on a person-to-person basis. The only contact she ever had with priests was from a distance. He on the altar, or in a car, or at a funeral. She never spoke to one on a one-to-one social basis. She never had any need to. Priests were strangers to her; not that they were strange, or odd, but they did not occupy a similar space as she, or other lay people, did. It wasn't, as far as she was concerned, that priests were on a pedestal, as that they seemed to exist on a separate universe or landscape. Her life concerns, her daily occupations and doings did not include men such as Father O'Byrne. So, his avoiding her eyes only confirmed her expectations. Of course they would avoid my eyes, or any layperson's eyes, for that matter. Was it not the case that they were trained in such a way as not to be allowed to speak to us as we would engage and speak to one another?

But why was that? Was it shyness on his part or his training that over the years moulded and formed him into the person she was now sitting opposite? Or, was it on the other hand, that he wished to show that he was non-partisan, that he was taking an objective approach to this particular problem?

Anne sensed that he wanted to look at her, wanted to engage in a more personable manner, but couldn't or wouldn't. It made her feel sorry for him. After all, her experience with men had been one of easy engagement, where they simply spoke and had normal conversations and normal feelings. Feelings which would, naturally, include attraction or its opposite, depending on circumstances. So, what feelings had she towards this priest, and what feelings, if any, did he have towards her? But it didn't matter. The issue was of a professional nature, not personal. On this occasion, he was stiff, formal, as, under the present circumstances, was unavoidable; but there was a hint of fear in his eyes, or at least a palpable discomfort.

"Thank you, Miss Connaughton for giving me your side of the story." He paused and looked out the window again.

"This is a most delicate situation. Strictly speaking you did hit him." He raised his hand anticipating her objection, "I know. I know you felt you had to in order to protect another student. This I accept." He turned to her, but not looking at her, he was addressing her at a spot on the table, "Mrs Dalton, is very upset."

"Naturally, Father."

"And, of course, as you might anticipate I have had complaints from young Kneafsey's parents. They are of the opinion that you did the right thing; that you protected their son from what could have been a very severe beating and they are also of the opinion that you are being treated unfairly by the principal, although, of course you realise that Miss O'Malley is in an invidious position."

Anne didn't agree. It was clear to her that she ought to be supporting and even fighting for Anne, instead of being afraid of a parent. But she said nothing. There was no point.

Father O'Byrne put his hands together as if he were at Mass and at the point of inviting his congregation to pray with him, "I have thought about this, and deliberated carefully, Miss Connaughton. I believe you did what you did in good faith; you did so, as you say, as you would with someone who was in an hysterical condition. I will relay my decision to Miss O'Malley." He stood, indicating the end of the meeting, "There is no question, Miss Connaughton, of you losing your job because of this incident. But might I remind you to be careful in future."

Anne stood with relief. "Thank you, Father. Of course there will be no repeat."

Anne left the priest's house knowing that the matter would not be taken further, which explained her relief, but she also left feeling sorry for Father O'Byrne. There was an isolation and a loneliness about him, but she reckoned that that was the price paid. She was sure there were compensations for him and for priests like him. She believed in God, and thus believed that God would somehow be the compensation they needed, and, she presumed, received. But that was something beyond her ken, and it was an area beyond her experience. She was content to be a teacher, loved being one, accepted that more than likely she would end up teaching for the rest of her life in a Catholic school, would, as per her own beliefs, as a Catholic, teach her children their prayers, their catechism, just as she was taught in her childhood, and as far as delving into the deeper theological questions, she was not really interested in journeying down that route, because, as far as she was concerned, her life was not making demands of her beyond where she found herself within the landscape of the present moment, and particular circumstance. So, from her point of view priests, such as Father O'Byrne, lived, or existed, in that different landscape than hers and her world, and would so remain.

However, as far as the reason for the interview with the school manager was concerned, the incident may have been forgotten about by the principal and the school manager, but it wasn't over for Mrs Dalton.

The problem with a small village, as Anne well knew, especially when you have little option but to do your shopping locally, is that you cannot avoid persons you wished you could avoid. Mrs Dalton was a case in point, and it would not have mattered if she were a mere housewife or farmer's wife, but she and her husband owned the local bar, grocery store and hardware shop, all under one roof. Avoiding someone like that was nigh impossible.

At first, Anne was reluctant to do her shopping in Garrydangan, but, as she discovered it was most inconvenient to have to cycle all the way to Clochdroode. Which she did, at least for the first few occasions, but two things forced her to reconsider. One, obviously, was distance and inconvenience, but the other was pride. She wasn't going to let herself be intimidated. She decided to take the bull by the horns, as it were, and go into Daltons to buy her bread, canned goods, sausages and rashers.

Mrs Dalton stood behind the counter, and gave Anne the eye as she entered. Mr Dalton was in the bar section pulling pints and serving whiskey to the local men.

"What are you doing, coming in here, with your hoity-toity ways?" Mrs Dalton challenged her, "You have some cheek coming in here after what you did to my child."

Mrs Daly, the priest's housekeeper, and Mrs Egan the widow who lived near her on the other side of the post-office, who were already in conversation with one another, stopped and watched for Anne's reaction. The two women weren't going to leave without seeing the outcome of this encounter. Their presence only emboldened Mrs Dalton. But it had a similar effect on Anne.

"I have come in here, as I have always, Mrs Dalton, to do my bit of shopping." She answered defiantly.

"Is that right, now, Missy Connaughton. Well, you can do your shopping somewhere else."

Anne looked at the two older women, who maintained as neutral a face as was possible. It was obvious that this scene would become the source of many stories in the village.

"My money is as good here as any other place, Mrs Dalton. And sure if you won't take it, I'm certain that Mr Dalton will be only too happy to have a few extra shillings in the till." Anne turned towards the bar, raising her voice, "Won't you, Mr Dalton?"

Frank Dalton came out of the bar section with a dish cloth in his hand. "What's up ladies?" He asked as he nervously wiped the counter, "Ah, Miss Connaughton, 'tis yourself."

"It is indeed, Mr Dalton." Anne looked at the two women who were still standing by the door, "I'm hoping I'll get better service from you than from what I'm getting here at the moment. Am I right, ladies?"

Frank nodded to his wife and indicated that there were some customers to be seen to in the bar. Mrs Dalton did not move. She was not pleased that her husband was not taking her side.

Frank Dalton turned to the men in the bar, "The Missus will be in to ye, lads," as he turned to Anne, "and what it is at all that I can get you, Miss Connaughton?"

Mrs Dalton huffed and pushed by her husband.

The two older ladies smiled at one another, "Isn't it a shocking grand day out there, now, thanks be to God." They turned to Frank, "Good day to you, Mr Dalton," and to Anne, "Miss Connaughton."

For some months following whenever Anne came into the shop, Mrs Dalton called to her husband to serve her. Maybe, as far as he was concerned, he realised his son was out of order. But Anne took a more cynical interpretation. She knew the senior Dalton well enough. He was a hard-nosed businessman. He could not afford to ignore Miss Connaughton, as she was popular in the village and neither could he afford to lose the Kneafseys and the other so-called 'migrant' families, as customers.

It was lucky for all concerned, including the Daltons, that the incident happened towards the end of Sixth class. It meant that Frankie had to leave primary school and go to the secondary. The next school year Frankie was sent to the Jesuit boarding school in Tullybeg. The school, and the village, was a calmer and quieter place as a result.

But he was home for the summer holidays, and already he was causing trouble. The sheep and the dead dog incident was yet another example. And now Anne's pupils would be asking her what happened yesterday. There was some trepidation in her heart and she wasn't at ease. It was going to be a difficult and tense day. What should she tell them?

She told them that bad men from Dublin are in the area and to be careful. But the truth was, of course, that the bad men were closer to them than they thought, and even more than she had thought. And, she reflected, recent events were bound to cause more trouble in the village. God only knew what it was going to lead to.

Chapter 4

Father Daniel O'Byrne was thankful to Tim Dooley, his sacristan, for taking him away from the Pattern Day football match melee. But as he drove back to the priest's house, he couldn't quite shake off the feeling that he was being cowardly. He ought to have intervened. He ought to have been, what he saw himself as being, the moral authority of his people. He had missed an opportunity to be a good, priestly influence over his flock. What he witnessed was a total shock to him. He had never expected that, what he had assumed were reasonable, rational men, they were all men, would descend to the level of savages. That was the very word he uttered to himself over and over again as he drove back to the house. In his imagination, he had only ever pictured some wild, pagan, African tribe behave in the manner he witnessed that very day.

He sat at his desk and went over in his mind what he should have done. He should have walked into the middle of the crowd, fearless, brandishing the cross, if not literally, at least metaphorically, exhorting his people to stop in the name of their God. They needed reminding of who they were, he should have stood in the middle of them, telling them, demanding that they kneel and pray for forgiveness. They were Catholics, Irishmen, not pagan savages, he should have berated them. He pictured himself a Saint Patrick, or better still, a fearless and stubborn Columbanus among the Gallic tribes and Chieftains, a man, if not converting the people to the true faith, at least reminding them of their baptism and their special and unique status as members, sons, of the Catholic Church. He should have shamed them in front of their womenfolk and their children.

At moments like this, when he was upset or confused, in need of succour and consolation he'd think of his mother Monica O'Byrne, and his spiritual mother, Mary the Blessed Mother. He would look to them for guidance. He was the second son of James T. O'Byrne, solicitor and businessman, late of Athlone and his wife, Monica. Being the second son was part of God's plan, he believed. If he had been the eldest, James junior, he would now be managing a solicitor's office in Athlone, the very same office and desk of his late father. James senior was not an expressive man, not a warm personality, but it was only when he was with James his oldest son, that he seemed happy. He regarded Daniel, as soft, too much a mother's boy. But his mother told him to hush, that Daniel was for the priesthood. For Monica O'Byrne, as with many mothers, to have a son in the Priesthood was a special grace and favour from God on her and her family. It demonstrated a special place not only in society, which was of course, in itself, highly important and even necessary, but also a sign of God's public acknowledgement as it were, of her family's position within the Catholic Church. To be the mother of a Catholic Priest was akin to a knighthood in England; she saw herself as part of an aristocracy, special and unique to Ireland, a true Irish aristocracy. He wasn't a Sir

Daniel O'Byrne, he was Father Daniel O'Byrne. So, whenever Daniel complained that his father ignored him in favour of his older brother, his mother would wipe his tears, if that were the case, or console him with the idea that he was more important than all the eldest sons in the country. He would be a priest of God, a jewel in the Crown of the Holy Roman Catholic Church. This was no mere idle fantasy, this was no fluffed up, puffed up, meaningless title; no, to his mother, and many Irish mothers, as Daniel realised, priesthood was a reality more real than the material reality of being a solicitor, or a businessman. In fact, the material reality of these other occupations and professions was a mere shadow, a mere fantasy compared to the spiritual reality of God and his representatives here on earth, His priests. His mother, Daniel sometimes mused, was more Platonic than Plato. And, as he sat in the dusking summer evening, his mind shivering and perseverating on the awful irrationality of what he had earlier witnessed, he was convinced that she was right. He was convinced that he had a duty, as their priest, to show them the true reality, the awesome reality that they were neglecting.

And now, at his desk, in his office, he would put together a homily to clearly outline his feelings and more importantly, the law of God.

And, so, on the following Sunday morning as he stood in the pulpit, he reminded his congregation of the power vested in him as their priest. He reminded them of his ordained privilege to be the only man in the church that morning who could change the bread and wine into the very body and blood of their Redeemer.

"And thus I speak to you this sacred morning, with the altar of sacrifice in front of your eyes, with the candles of the light of God lit reminding you of his command to be a light to all nations; and I stand here as your priest who will shortly bring forth the Real Presence of Jesus Christ, God's only begotten son, to say to you that you have disgraced yourselves. Not only disgraced yourselves before the Crucified Christ but in front of our visitors and fellow parishioners from Clochdroode; but, it seems I have to remind you, that your actions were spoken of to a wider field, I mean of course, the Protestants who, though they may not have been actually there, but, no doubt will have heard, and who will now be snickering and laughing at us. See how these Roman Catholics behave, they will say to one another in their parlours and in their Chapels. See how we have become a laughingstock. This must never happen again. This must be expunged from our parish. You who were involved in such acts of beastliness and savagery must repent. And (he paused and looked out at every section of the Church, but with especial emphasis to the men to the left of the aisle), I expect to be hearing from you in the Confessional, where there, and only there, can I as Christ's representative, grant you absolution. I do not want to be in this pulpit again, in some future time, admonishing you for your sins. Sins. Yes, sins, for you have sinned. You have broken the law of God, you have committed the sin of scandal, you have led astray your children, by your behaviour you have given them bad example, and what did Christ Jesus say to those who would lead His children astray. Yes, my dear people, let me remind you. 'It would be better that a millstone were hanged about his neck and he cast into the sea'."

Father Daniel O'Byrne had hoped his words would have impact. Many of his parishioners came to him afterwards, or stopped him on the street, and thanked him for his sermon. When he went into the post office to buy stamps and post letters, Josie Fagan said to him, "Fair play to you, Father. No harm for them to hear what you were saying. A disgrace the way some people behave in this parish. And many of them not here a wet week. Coming in from God knows where, into this nice quiet village and causing trouble."

Mrs McDonagh, who had come into the church to light a candle for a special intention, whispered that it was time 'these people heard the truth, too much resentment and hypocrisy in these parts, Father'.

Father O'Byrne was delighted with the compliments, and was filled with a glow of satisfaction, as he thought of his mother and how proud she would have been if she had been sitting in the congregation.

But no one came to confession, not one of the men whom he knew were involved, came to the sacrament to seek God's forgiveness. Did his words have no effect whatsoever on these guilty men? What good was it to be complimented by the good people, all women of the parish, who did nothing wrong? It was a slap in the face to the Church, an act of unacceptable defiance, for them to refuse to avail of the sacrament of forgiveness.

And what was he to make of Dalton's dog and what happened to Keane's sheep? He had met Garda John Holton when he visited Clochdroode. They happened to meet as Father O'Byrne was getting out of his car to go into Cloonans Hardware and Electrical. John Holton was in full uniform. They naturally fell into conversation and after the initial greetings and talk of how grand the weather was, Father O'Byrne asked him about what had happened.

"A bad business, Father, a bad business, entirely. Not that it doesn't happen. With stray dogs and farm animals, things can happen. You know yourself."

What the priest learned was that Dalton's dog, Dodger, managed to slip out and escape from the yard, late in the night or early in the morning. And, as dogs do, especially terriers, he attacked Keane's sheep and killed it.

"But the dog," the priest enquired indignantly, "how, in the name of God did it end up hanging by its neck in a tree, John?"

"Well, to be honest we don't know the truth of that, Father. But what the Keane's told us was that it heard the sheep in distress, ran out with their shotgun to find out what was the matter. It's the way with farmers, you know. Animal stock is stock. It's their livelihood. They were perfectly in their rights to protect their stock, Father."

He was disappointed in the attitude of the Garda. How could they allow such a thing to happen? It wouldn't have been so bad if the Keane's had made a complaint to the Guards and let them deal with it. They had the authority to put the dog down. But to permit this act of violence, in front of everyone, even the children, in such a public manner, was surely undermining the rule of law.

"Yes, yes. Of course, John, but hanging it, and in front to their shop and for all to see, that's not right. What are we the Wild West?"

Garda Holton lifted his hands, as if to say, there was no explaining what some people would do. "A message was sent.

It's the way of the farmer. He won't brook any threat to his livelihood. Stock is sacrosanct."

"And what about the Daltons?"

"Ah, sure the young lad will get a new dog. Look Father, it was their dog what killed the sheep. They know that. They're in the wrong. He has to control his dog. It's as simple as that. And you know Frank Dalton, he's not going to make too much of a fuss over a bloody dog, especially when he knows that he daren't alienate his customers. It's a loss he can handle. He needs the Keanes, the Heneghans and the Tarpeys of this world, Father. Business is business."

Father O'Byrne finally relented. It wasn't an issue for the Church, or he, as a priest, to get involved in. The law of God was not being broken; it was the natural law. An animal for an animal. He was disappointed in the Garda's attitude. But, as far as he was concerned, it was the slippery slope. The law cannot be taken into laymen's hands. There were authorities and institutions of state that must uphold civil behaviour and morality.

Chapter 5

Doreen Heneghan spread out a bolt of cloth on the counter. "This is just gorgeous, Anne. Feel that."

Anne admired the lightness yet strength of the cloth, she could picture a perfect summer dress, the reds, whites and pinks in a modern rose pattern sent a burst of delight through her.

"And," Doreen bent down to pull out a wooden box which was kept under the counter, flicked though envelopes of paper patterns until she selected the one she was looking for, "here is a new pattern, just come in."

Anne's eyes lit up, "Wow, Doreen, this looks something like what Ava Gardner would wear."

The two friends shared a passion for dressmaking. Anne had a Singer sewing machine and a work-top in her rented cottage. Doreen and herself spent many evenings cutting and stitching, as they drank tea, ate Doreen's scones and just chatted with one another as they worked.

Doreen was the only child of Seamus and Mary Heneghan who came from Erris, in the beautiful wilds of west Mayo, to their new Land Commission farm in Garrydangan. But it was proving a difficult task to make a living here. Having no sons to help work the farm was a setback in itself, though Doreen and her mother helped as much as they could around the farm, but Seamus' health was never robust enough to make a real success of farming. He suffered from asthma and, while he could work through it, there were times when it was too debilitating to be able to make the living he wished. Their neighbours, the Keanes and the Tarpeys, who also came from Mayo at around the same time, and Kilroys, who had farmed in the area for generations, were a great help and they made sure the Heneghan turf was in and the hay saved, but it meant that Seamus, Mary and Doreen had to reciprocate. The *meithil* system of cooperation kept the farm going but the asthma was not improving. It meant that Doreen had to find ways to supplement the family income. Doreen found it easy to get jobs working in local shops as she was always in good humour and had a ready smile for customers. She was hardworking, honest and had an ability to deal with difficult customers. She had been working for McElroys, & Sons, Draperies, of Clochdroode for about a year when Anne had been appointed the new teacher in Garrydangan. It was while Anne was shopping in McElroy's for cloth to make a dress for work that the young women found that they shared an interest in fashion and dressmaking. Their friendship developed and they became as close as sisters. Anne was the sister Doreen never had, and Doreen, easy-going and of a sunny personality, was the only person in Garrydangan who was of a similar age and who was not a mother or sister of any of her pupils.

When Anne had finished her business in McElroy's, both women agreed to meet in Scully's Tearoom later.

Miss Scully, the elegantly dressed owner of her clean and well-appointed premises, served them her special fresh home-baked scones and placed a China pattern pot of tea on the table, smiling at two of her favourite customers, "Always nice to see you ladies, looking so glamorous in this dull old town." She pointed to the scones, "I'm trying a new recipe for my fruit scones, so please, let me know what you think."

The two young women said they would be delighted to.

After Doreen poured the tea and was buttering her scone, she told Anne she had some news.

"Not bad news, I hope."

"The farm isn't going well, Anne. You know that."

Anne stopped drinking her tea, fearful she knew what she was about to hear.

"We're thinking of selling up and moving to England." Doreen said simply. It was better to get bad news out and done with quickly.

"Ah, no, don't tell me you're leaving." Anne felt the loss already. She tried desperately to hide her disappointment, she didn't want to make things harder on Doreen, but neither did she want to be thinking of the pain she would be feeling at her going away.

Doreen tried to brush away tears but did not succeed. "I know. I know. I can't believe it, but it was bound to happen."

"How? Why?" Anne had her handkerchief out and was squeezing it in her hand.

"Ach, sure Dad was never a farmer. I know he has asthma and all, but to be honest, he was never cut out for farming. He got an opportunity to get out of Erris and he took it because he knew if he didn't, he'd be stuck there for the rest of his life. He tried to make a go of it here, but his heart was never in it."

"But, what are ye going to do?"

"His brother, my uncle Tom, has a business in Birmingham. He buys houses and does them up and resells them. He says he needs a man to help him. Da is a real good carpenter, sure you know yourself, he's made all the chairs and tables for the house."

Ann had admired the handiwork; it was tasty work.

"But Tom wants him to help him run the business," Doreen continued, "do the carpentry work, be a kind of foreman and then move on to the next house. Tom says there's a boom in the building trade over there in England."

"What's going to happen the farm?"

"He'll sell up and go."

"But who's is going to buy it?"

Both women knew that selling a farm in Garrydangan wasn't necessarily a straightforward affair. Anne, though from Tipperary and of farming background, had never experienced the deep hatreds and divisions she saw in this county when it came to Land Commission farms. She knew that when it became public that the Heneghans were going to sell up and leave, locals would not take kindly to another outsider coming in and buying a farm they felt they had a right to. What surprised, and even annoyed, her was that it didn't seem to matter that the very locals who would be complaining weren't interested in the farm, or any farm, but, to them, the fact that someone they didn't know or someone they felt deserved the land would not get it, galled them, to the point of anger and even sometimes, violence. This wasn't something theoretical or hidden away so that civilised living was made possible but, as Anne saw, the Pattern Day football match and the trouble afterwards proved that it was very much real and raw. It all surfaced that day.

"Tomás Keane is interested," Doreen said.

"That sounds reasonable," Anne nodded, "It makes sense. It's next to his. It'll give him a chance to make a bigger farm so Michael can take it over."

"Yes, but it's not as simple as that. Da has been keeping his cards close to his chest. You know how he is with money. He's going to want a good price. Even though himself and Tomás are close, they're not so close that Da will let him have it for nothing. So, it's going to depend on whether or not Tomás will be able to get a loan from the bank. That's going to cause problems because it's not certain sure that he would get the loan. And anyway, even if he does, when it comes to the auction you never know if he'll be outbid."

"But by who? If Tomás can get the loan he has as good a chance as anyone."

Doreen looked around the Tearoom. It was a busy place this time of day. Miss Scully was hovering around from table to table, chatting and greeting the customers and seating new ones. What she had to say was not for public ears. "Let's finish this up and go outside. I can't talk here."

Both women stood to leave, and Miss Scully turned to them, "Leaving us already, ladies," she smiled, "what did you think of my new recipe?"

Anne and Doreen smiled sweetly, "They were lovely, Miss Scully."

"Delighted to hear it. Well, thanks for coming and sure we'll see you again."

They sat on the low wall across from St Michael's parish church. A grey Massey Ferguson trundled down towards the centre of Clochdroode and one of Doreen's customers, the elderly Miss Egan, recognised her and waved as she passed on her bicycle.

Anne waited for Doreen to speak.

"That's just the thing. Who is going to make a bid for it?" Doreen put her hand on Anne's arm, "Anne you must keep this under your hat and swear you'll never repeat it."

Anne was taken aback. She wasn't comfortable with secrets and conspiracies and was about to say that maybe she oughtn't to know. That it was better that she didn't know, and whatever happens, happens and it was all in God's hands anyway. But at the same time she couldn't help wanting to know.

"Our farm is beside the Esker quarry."

"So?"

"Da thinks that there is someone who is interested in buying the farm in order to have access to it and use the farm, or the fields by the quarry as an entry way and a place to set up an office and have trucks coming in and out."

"That sounds like a good idea," Anne said, "sure, won't it give employment to the area."

"Yeah, but if the Keane's find out they'll object, and the farm won't sell."

"But who wants to buy it and set up a quarry business?"

"I don't know."

"Does your father know?"

"Again, I don't know. He's not saying anything to me or Mam. And maybe he doesn't know. Maybe it'll be a ghost buyer."

"A what?"

"Some local with money, or even outsider, might buy it on behalf of a client, who then takes it over."

"Can they do that?"

"Why not? Money is money, and if you have it you can do what you like."

Anne could see that at the end of the day, as far as the Heneghans were concerned, they wanted the best price, no matter who bought, and they were not sentimental about who took over. If the Keanes could not get the money together, no matter how good a neighbour they were, the Heneghan farm would not be added to the Keane farm. Their future was in England. Their prospects looked good. England was booming, and a lot of Irish, including locals, were leaving looking for work on the buildings and roadways.

But, this did not matter. Anne felt a stab of pain. She would be losing Doreen. Her eyes became wet with tears. But she had to suppress them, otherwise both of them would have collapsed into one another's arms sobbing, right here in public. And what good would that do? It wouldn't change anything. She would just have to put up with it.

Chapter 6

Frank Dalton made it his business to know Captain Hubert Tyrrell, and more especially, Captain Tyrrell's business. Captain Tyrrell was the nephew of Lady Tyrrell. A Devereaux from Wexford, as Dalton discovered. Lady Constance wasn't one born into the English aristocratic, or any aristocratic line. She was an actress, it was said, who had small parts in the Abbey and who later, during the Great War, ended up walking or dancing on the boards of the West End. Whatever Devereaux she hailed out of it wasn't from a family of silver spoons and horse stables; and whatever way it happened, her journey led to the position of wife to Sir Garnett Holmes-Tyrrell of the Barony of Clochdroode, and the occupier of Tyrrell House. She had no children and, from sources close to the ear of Frank Dalton, Captain Tyrrell, her only living relative, was the sole heir.

Up to six months ago Mr Denis Giles was the manager of Tyrrell House and overseer of its land and properties. Rent was paid to Mr Giles at the Gate Lodge each month. Besides the house and land, much of it sold to the Land Commission, the Tyrrells owned property in the village of Garrydangan. The line of houses on the church side of the village down to the river, which included the Post Office, Mrs Daly's, the parish housekeeper, the house Miss Connaughton the primary school teacher rented, and two derelict sites, once occupied by O'Briens and Higgins' were also owned by the Tyrrells.

When Denis Giles retired, Captain Tyrrell took over the managing of all properties and holdings. To Frank Dalton's surprise and delight, the Captain was no dry stick, like Giles. He made a point, at the end of rent day, to pay his respects to Dalton in the bar, order a whiskey and Guinness and sit quietly reading The Irish Field, with pencil in hand, deciding who to back at Leopardstown, the Curragh, or of course, Cheltenham.

Dalton was loath, at first, to disturb his studies, but quickly found out that he was, unlike many an English country gent, an affable and sociable type; and he soon learnt that Captain Tyrrell had recently retired from the British Army after a spell in India. "Gandhi did us out of a job, Mr Dalton," Tyrrell said ruefully over a second whiskey, on the house, "and it coincided with my time to call it a day with regard to my military service to his Majesty."

Dalton was impressed with the army man, liked 'the cut of him', as he told his customers when the conversation turned to Captain Tyrrell and the Tyrrell House, and fortune. The Captain dressed like a military man should, complete with tweed waistcoat, starched linen shirt and tie, and on his feet a stout pair of brown, daily shined, brogues. You can't beat military training, Dalton would tell anyone willing to listen, it stays with you for a lifetime.

It was perfect timing as far as Dalton was concerned. He had, he told his wife, what turned out to be a most efficacious conversation with the Captain, after Dalton served both himself and the Captain a few more rounds on the house.

This 'most efficacious conversation' took place only about two months ago. The Captain came in as usual, took his place by the now well-stoked fire, with a hot whiskey on the table. Dalton sidled over to him and greeted him with an offer of another whiskey and moved the topic, as pre-planned on Dalton's, and his wife's, part, to a question about the old derelict properties.

"Sure, they look shockin' bad there in the village, Captain." Dalton said, "Sure wouldn't they be a grand source of revenue if you did them up. I'd say there are many the people would be interested in renting."

"Do you think so, Mr Dalton?"

"Not stepping on your toes or delving anywhere into your own private business, Captain, but I do be thinking that it's a waste to be having two fine properties there empty and not getting a red farthing out of them."

"You know, Mr Dalton," he said sipping his whiskey, "I was thinking the same. In fact, when I came here, on behalf of my aunt, I was surprised to see that Mr Giles hadn't done anything about them."

This was music to Dalton. He knew he was dealing with a like-minded man. This Captain Tyrrell was no gentleman farmer, or at least a gentleman landowner who, like his English counterparts looked down on the merchant class, of which Dalton considered himself to be a proud member. He had learnt something in India, no doubt, where the art of business was developed to a highly sophisticated level. Or else he was true blood of the Devereaux (if that was her real name; there were rumours), one hard-working actress, or whatever, and one who knew a penny from a pound; and this man, in Dalton's estimation, knew how to bend and spend a penny. He was hoping that the Captain knew how to make a penny into a pound, and many more from where they came from.

Another piece of luck (or was it fate?), was a piece of information which John Holton had gleaned from Garda sources in Dublin. Lady Constance owned a townhouse in Rathmines and through her solicitor it came to the attention of Holton's sources that the Tyrrells were in debt. Revenues from holdings, along with new tax laws, plus an expensive lifestyle, meant that Lady Tyrrell could not continue to live in the luxury with which she was accustomed, that is, without a serious input of cash, or at least an opportunity to increase cash flow. Once again Dalton saw his chance. He slowly, patiently and quietly developed a plan. He drew Garda John Holton into this plan and both men sized up their man and his present circumstance and saw an opportunity. And this particular evening would be the first step in achieving their goal.

Frank Dalton told John Holton to come into the bar at around the same day and time as the Captain and to sit by him, chat and talk about horses or whatever interested the Captain. The Curragh festival would be an ideal topic to warm things up, to which Holton obliged. This part of the plan went on for a few weeks, and then, on cue, Dalton joined them and invited the Captain and Holton into his sitting room. Much tea, Margaret's sandwiches and sweet cake were applied, with the washing down thereof with whiskey and good conversation, which led to the moment where a business opportunity he might be interested in, was put before him. As it turned out, and to both men's delight, the Captain was ready to listen.

Over a bottle of Jameson Crested Ten, Dalton put forward the proposal. A certain property had come on the market, he informed the English man. This particular property was adjacent to a quarry, or a gravel pit. This pit had massive potential. There was a building boom taking place in Ireland, he informed the Captain. The government was investing in new houses outside many of the larger towns. This, of course, meant there would be a huge demand for sand, gravel, pipes and roof-tiles. The quarry in question was on Tyrrell property, but the only viable access to it was through a particular farm.

The Captain showed no hesitation, "And what would you bring to the venture?"

Dalton and Holton smiled at one another, nodding their mutual agreement that here, in fact, was a mind that knew business. They had him hooked.

"Well, Captain, it so happens that we, my good wife and I, have a piece of land, given to us by her father, which we are willing to sell as an investment. And, if we play our cards right, John here," Dalton indicated the smiling, self-satisfied, Holton who, a teetotaller, was still drinking tea and eating sandwiches, "will provide the political clout needed."

"What do you mean 'political clout'?"

"Well, Captain, it so happens that local elections are due early next year. Our present councillor, Jamesie McGawley, rather conveniently, is retiring. John here, is not only the secretary of the local GAA club, he is also the chair of the local Cumann Fianna Fail. Now, Fianna Fail, are the natural party of power in this country. They are not in power at the moment, but the present shower are so bad, there is nothing surer but we'll be back in power very soon. John here will put himself forward, and no doubt, get the nomination and, when the elections are called will be well placed to win. After all, he'll get the McGawley Fianna Fail vote, but he's certain sure to get the GAA vote as well."

"And why would this be important?"

"Two words, Captain." Dalton smiled benignly, "Planning permission. We buy the farm. Put in an application for the right of way to the quarry; you, as owner of the quarry, place an application for a business to excavate the quarry and a business plan to produce sand and gravel. We'd be a team."

"I've a few bob put away myself," John Holton added. "I'm due to retire from the Guards. I'll have a bit of a pension I can, er, invest. We're all winners."

The Captain rolled the golden whiskey glass in his hand. "Let me think about it, gentlemen. Let me think about it."

"No hurry, Captain, but we'll need to be moving on the farm as soon as possible."

Dalton and Holton shook the Captain's hand as he left, "Needless to say, under your hat. Under your hat."

Tyrrell nodded, conspiratorially, "Of course. Will be in touch."

After the men had left and his wife upstairs in bed, Dalton sat in the darkening sitting room, sipping his favourite Powers whiskey. His dream was becoming a reality. He had married late in life, but he had married well. Margaret Mills was the eldest in her family, and only sister to two younger brothers. It was her curse to be born a girl, she had often told her husband. "Had I been a son and the eldest I would have had a right sizable farm to my name." But she was close to her father. In fact, she was the favourite, but law was law and land was land. She couldn't inherit. The boys, after all, had the Mills name. But by way of compensation, and to the chagrin of Trevor, the eldest boy, Margaret was given a piece of land, and it was this land that would be sold to invest in the Heneghan farm. He thanked God that Doreen was a girl and their only child, and that Heneghan's failure to make a living from the farm would be his opportunity for success. He thanked God, also, that he had a son. His mother may not be the best, she was too soft on him had spoilt him, but he'd come around. He'd grow out of it. Become a man.

When he got things up and running, he mused, when he and his partners were pulling together, he would leave a legacy, a thriving business for his only son. He lifted his glass of whiskey in salute to his dreams. The Dalton's of Garrydangan would live long in the memory, they would be the family in the area, they would replace the Tyrrells and then the time would come, maybe not in his life time but surely in Frankie's, Tyrrell House would be theirs. Dalton House. He and Margaret liked the ring of that. They would be the new aristocracy. The new money. The new family in power. He finished his drink. Who knows where the dream could end!

Chapter 7

When Anne Connaughton went in to the Lodge office to pay her rent, she was expecting Denis Giles to be behind the high oak counter. Mr Giles, as that was always how she greeted him, was a tall, slim, slightly stooped elderly gentleman, with, what Anne described as having skin the colour of an old school roll book. Instead, she found herself greeting a tall, neatly dressed, military man. Anne thought of him as a military man before she found out he was indeed an ex-army officer. He was sitting behind the long deal table, examining the pages of the large, green leather covered rent book.

"Good morning," he greeted with a businessman's smile. He had navy blue eyes, light sandy hair, balding, and Anne noted almost immediately a nick in his right ear, as if it had been cut, or nipped by some sharp object.

"I'm looking for Mr Giles," Anne said, indicating her rent book.

"Well, I'm sorry to say Mr Giles has recently retired. I can deal with that." He stood and came over to the counter and placed one hand on the counter and the other outstretched to accept Anne's rental book.

His hands were large, his nails manicured and had light blonde hairs on the back. He moved quickly and with confidence, checking Anne's name off the register, counting her money, writing out a receipt and handing it to her. She wanted to ask how Mr Giles was, and inquire into his retirement, but Anne was intimidated by him. He wasn't the type to engage in small talk. Anne and Captain Tyrrell nodded to one another as she put the book into her handbag. She said good day and left.

Snooty ex-English soldier, she said to herself, as she walked back to her house annoyed that she was too shy to enquire after Mr Giles and tell him to tell Mr Giles that she was asking for him.

Over the next few weeks, mostly through Josie Fagan in the post-office next door, she learnt that Captain Hubert Tyrrell was Lady Tyrrell's nephew, that he had been in India, had been involved in some skirmishes with the local Hindus and Muslims and had something to do with the transition to Indian independence. He retired from the army and had come to Ireland to live with, or work on behalf of, his aunt.

"And what about Mr Giles?" Anne asked.

"Sure, didn't they retire him, poor man." Josie lowered her voice to a conspiratorial whisper, which was her normal mode of conversation, "No respect for old age, at all, at all. They say (which meant she had been listening into phone calls and had gleaned, or rather excavated, local gossip) that he's living with his sister in Clochdroode. Pensioned him off, they did."

On subsequent months when Anne conducted her business at the Lodge Office, the Captain had thawed out, as Anne would say. He may have just been a naturally shy man. But he had a wonderful smile, when he allowed himself to do so. He came across as reticent and distant, but, Anne imagined, if you got him talking about a topic he was interested in, his time in the army, for instance, he might actually be an interesting person. On the rare occasions, they might meet in the village, or when she might see him come out of Daltons he'd raise his hand in salute, in army gesture and greet her with a, Good day, Miss Connaughton. Anne blushed, which galled her, and she'd return the greeting with 'Captain' and a nod of her head and walk on.

She liked him. Her heart fluttered when she saw him. She didn't admit it at first, because she was the kind of young woman who believed herself to be in command of her feelings, especially romantic ones; but it came to the point where there was no use denying it, but would only allow herself to acknowledge whatever admiration lay on the surface. She liked his military style, his tweed waist coat, his neatly fitting shirt and tie, his brown polished shoes. His bearing was of a man confident of his place in the world; he projected the mien of a man of life experience who was not overwhelmed by the bad and evil of the world around him, but had somehow, through pain, made an accommodation to it. He seemed, to Anne, to exude an attractive maturity she rarely saw in men, at least in her experience. She acknowledged she was a relevant innocent. A daughter of a small farmer, who was bright, intelligent, had a happy disposition, was a quick learner and had a genuine desire to be a teacher. And she was lucky enough, or had worked hard enough, to achieve a County Council scholarship to train in Carysfort and to land herself, on the first attempt, as a teacher in Garrydangan.

And meeting this man only highlighted, and exacerbated, her own feelings of youth and ignorance. She never had a boyfriend. She was too busy, her mother said, to give the time of day to any lad that showed any interest. Carysfort was an all-women institution, there was little opportunity to meet and study with men of her age, and while she had male friends, usually friends of her brothers, which didn't really count, and on occasion, rare though it was, she did manage to slip the shackles the holy Sisters imposed on their charges and 'jump the wall' on a Friday or Saturday night; but she was seen as being too 'brainy for boys' and she even heard one of the lads calling her a 'blue-stocking'. She didn't know what it meant, and when she did find out she was quite proud of the sobriquet. She was a bit of an intellectual, and she did indeed read a lot. But she was also creative. Her mother did all the knitting at home, and encouraged young Anne to make dresses. It, after all, saved money and you always knew that what Anne made it was certain to fit, and after a few early disasters, look well.

But men? Well, she could take them or leave them. Her life as a teacher in Garrydangan was too busy, too energy-sapping to have room for chasing, or being chased by the sons of farmers or shopkeepers of Garrydangan or Clochdroode. And, anyway, there was no one in Garrydangan or Clochdroode, nor between both, who took her fancy. She was not the type to allow any man to sweep her off her feet, or for her to be swept off in some Mills & Boon romantic fit.

Not until now. And knowing that, Anne was no self-deceiver, she was too practical a young woman for that, she came to a decision. She wasn't going to show any indication that she liked this Captain. Whenever she went into the Lodge Office, or happened to see him in the village, or even in Clochdroode, or even, if it went as far as that, Athlone, she would keep her greetings or social interactions totally on an impersonal and professional level. This decision was based on her belief that 'if it was to be it would be'. In other words, she would not actively pursue the desire for special intimacies, or love, she would wait for these active desires to pursue her. This attitude gave her a sense of protection and security, Fate would deal her hand for her.

But it was difficult to adhere to these prescriptions, especially when he showed such solicitude regarding her rented accommodation. Each time she entered the office to pay the rent he asked her was there anything she needed? Was the furniture, the chairs and tables 'to her liking and requirements?' If the bedroom furniture needed changing, including the mattress, he said he could very well understand her desire to have them removed, as he 'quite understood how long these items had been in the house'.

He made an offer that whenever she had a school holiday and she was away for any reason he would get a painter in to 'redo the place'.

She told him that she was grateful for his kindness and his thoughtfulness that she was quite happy with everything and that as far as she was concerned there was no need for any changes to her room or kitchen.

Anne appreciated his solicitude, his un-intrusive solicitude. He was careful not to overstep his position, she noted. He was tactful, saying that he was thankful to have a renter who was trustworthy and paid on time and did not make unnecessary demands on him as the landlord, and after each enquiry he reminded her that if there was anything he could do to let him know.

Anne, after each meeting, was left with the impression that he liked her. But she wasn't going to soften her approach.

He was her landlord. He was a lot older than she, he must have been in his late thirties; she was, she again admitted, a little intimidated by him. Even if they did 'go out' or happened to meet in a 'social' occasion, she feared she wouldn't be able to engage in any long, or meaningful conversation with him as she was totally useless when it came to 'small talk'. It was a strain even to think about it, so she admitted it, accepted the unlikelihood of any such 'date' or occasion, and put is behind her.

On a late October evening after school, Anne was in her front room, her 'working room' as she called it. She was placing a paper pattern on a beautiful piece of cloth that would be just right for Doreen. It was to be a summer dress. She pictured Doreen in it and smiled. Doreen was so tall and elegant, had such beautiful flowing red hair. This dress would look wonderful on her, the various shades of green would highlight her fair skin.

It was getting to be late in the evening and she continued to work under the electric light. She was so engrossed in her cutting and fitting that she did not, at first, hear a noise at the back. Then a few minutes later she heard something being knocked over. It sounded like the bin, or the rusted garden chair. She listened again to the night's silence and was happy that it must have been a cat or a dog. She continued to work for about another half an hour when she felt too tired to do any more. She'd better stop, or else she'd make mistakes. Anyway, it was time for bed.

Her bedroom was at the back. The moon bathed the room in soft grey light and then darkened when a heavy black cloud slid by.

Anne brushed her hair at the dressing table. The light was on. She brushed vigorously, not looking at herself in the mirror, but only checking intermittently that her hair was smoothing out and was ready to be tied up for bed. And, as was her habit, she turned out the light and undressed. She went over to the window to pull the curtains. There was someone spying on her. She sensed it, was sure of it. She pulled the curtains together and then opened them slightly to get a better look. Her stomach tensed with anger and fear. The garden was long and narrow. Just below her were two iron garden chairs facing out towards the garden and an old kitchen table that was rotting and full of woodworm. Her eyes adjusted to the darkness and just as the moon managed to peek through a series of light clouds, she could make out a figure. It was Frankie Dalton. She'd know the shape of his head anywhere. He was hiding behind the dilapidated wooden tool shed. As soon as he realised he was spotted he slid off on his stomach like a soldier in a trench. Anne could hear him knock over something. It must have been a hoe or spade that was leaning up against the garden wall.

Anne was so upset she ran over to the light switch and turned on the light. She found it difficult to breathe and she was crying. It annoyed her to be crying. She sat on her bed and pulled the blankest around her, using the sheet to dry her eyes.

"The dirty bastard," she said to herself. She felt humiliated, exposed. It was as if her room wasn't there, that the walls had come down and she was sitting on her bed with the whole world looking at her, watching her every move. She had no privacy at all. The whole of Garrydangan could have seen her getting ready for bed. He must have been there most of the evening. He had been waiting for her to get to her room, was watching her as she brushed her hair, saw her as she undressed. She wished Doreen was with her. She wouldn't be able to sleep. Never had she felt so alone, never so isolated, or so exposed. She wrapped the blanket tighter and lay down on the floor in a foetal position.

She pictured him on the shed, waiting, like a robber, to make sure no one would catch him. She was sure he was laughing at her, she had a picture in her mind of him making fun of her, saying to her, I can do anything I want and there is nothing you can do about it. He could do what he liked. She moved closer to the bed and crouched behind it to make sure no one could see her from the outside. She wished her mother was here. She wished she was back home where she could run into her parents room, as she did so often as a child when she was frightened by thunder and lightning, or had a bad dream, or for some reason was too scared to sleep. She wished she was a child again when there was somebody to protect her. But there was nobody.

The next day was a school day. There was no question of her taking a day off school. She would act as she usually did; she would be Miss Connaughton, schoolteacher. She wouldn't say a word of what happened to anyone, especially Louise O'Malley. All she would do would be to shake her snobby head and say nothing, or she would tell her to just get on with it. And maybe she was right. There was nothing to do. She just had to get on with it. Teach her times-tables, her Gaeilge, reading, and the catechism.

But all day long she couldn't get the image of Frankie Dalton lying on the shed spying on her, leering at her, out of her mind. She tried to brush it away, but it kept coming back.

By lunchtime, she was exhausted. She had been irritable with the children. She complained more when they didn't give the right answer. They knew there was something wrong. She knew by the way they looked at her, watched her every move, fearful that they would upset her. She decided that as a treat, as a way of making it up to them, she would allow them to do drawing for the rest of the day. They'd like that.

"And now children, I want you to take out your pencils and crayons. I will hand out sheets for you to draw." The smiles on their faces gave her a lift.

During what would have been the last period of the day, Miss O'Malley came to the room. The children froze, anticipating what was going to happen.

"I'm hearing a lot of noise in here," she looked sharply at the children and turned a critical eye to Anne, "surely, Miss Connaughton, the children would be better off learning the prayers and responses for their First Holy Communion."

Anne found it difficult to hold her temper, "Ah, Miss O'Malley," she said as brightly as she could manage, "the children have been so well behaved, I thought it…"

But she didn't get a chance to finish. Miss O'Malley turned away from the class and banged the door. The children gave a jump and then after they felt it was safe, they continued to draw and chat among themselves.

Anne turned to the window tried her best to control her breathing. She could feel a tear forming around her eye. She brushed it away. 'Bitch'. She mumbled to herself. She wasn't sure if any of the children heard.

Chapter 8

Father Daniel O'Byrne knelt at the *pre dieu* to prepare his mind for the celebration of the Eucharist. Tim Dooley quietly and reverently was laying out the vestments in the manner he had learnt as a postulant for the Christian Brothers. Father O'Byrne knew very little about his sacristan other than he was employed by the previous parish priest, Father James O'Donnell, many years ago and that Tim was not a person to divulge any information about himself. Father O'Byrne appreciated his quiet efficiency, his punctuality and sense of duty to the parish and its priests. Besides not knowing that his sacristan had been a postulant, Father O'Byrne did not know that Tim had left the Christian Brothers due to ill health. He had spent some time in a sanatorium to treat his TB, and afterwards his doctors told him, quite bluntly, that he would never be able for the classroom, and the Brothers advised that he leave Religious Life. What Father O'Byrne did know was that Tim lived with his sister, Josie Fagan, above the post office, that he smoked heavily, despite ill health, and was an avid follower of Gaelic football, and attended every club and county game.

Father O'Byrne prayed before his Mass that he would be worthy of his calling to the priesthood and that God would help him and be at his side as he celebrated the sacred mystery of the Eucharist. As he reverently put on his vestments Tim made sure the cruets of water and wine were placed on the altar, and that the Missal was placed on the altar and that the altar boys behaved themselves and were in a right frame of mind to serve at Father O'Byrne's Mass.

St Joseph's wasn't the main parish church. It served the people of Garrydangan and the outlying farms. It was a relatively small church with a capacity of about two to three hundred people. Father O'Byrne, after he read the gospel reading for the day, turned to the people to give his homily. It was the only time he faced his congregation, and for him it was the most distracting. As he turned to face the people he already knew where Anne Connaughton would be sitting and he consciously avoided looking for her or being seen to look at her.

He prayed silently for custody of the eyes. It was part of the Maynooth training. He and his class were told repeatedly by the dean of studies and by the retreat masters who came on annual retreat, to avoid the company of women. They were, as priests working in a parish, to keep interactions with women short and business-like. They were to form the habit of avoiding their eyes and to keep their own eyes three feet in front as they walked in public. It was clear that failing to follow these precepts was to fall into the occasion of sin.

His understanding of sexual matters, and even the sexual act to bring about conception, was confined to one lecture on how babies were conceived, but that was only in the context of the theology of the Immaculate Conception. His only other instruction on sex education came from jokes made by some seminarians who, he found, were crude, even loutish, and, in time, he noted, these were the very ones who left the seminary before ordination; the other way he learned was from his female parishioners who came to make their confessions. Even in these cases, he learned very little and even that little was vague and confusing.

It shamed and embarrassed him to recall his first time preaching in front of his Garrydangan parishioners and how he first caught sight of Anne Connaughton and was astounded at how beautiful she was and how her green eyes, like deep emeralds, seemed to pierce through him. He immediately looked away blushing, ashamed that she had noticed. He had seen many women before, obviously, he had seen beautiful women in the films and in the magazines and books, which was unsettling in itself, but to see beauty, in the flesh, as it were, was a completely different kind of experience. Anne Connaughton's beauty wasn't a film star type of beauty that was distant and inaccessible; Anne was something different, she was unsettlingly close and real, and vibrant, too vibrant for his comfort. She had a clear, neatly structured oval face, and eyes that announced intelligence and strength of character; she was medium sized, slim build and dressed neatly and fashionably but not showy. It was understated but it was a statement, nonetheless.

It was when he visited her class to begin the preparation for First Holy Communion that he was overwhelmed by her. He had never experienced anything like that before in his life. It was the way she smiled at the children, made them feel special and loved. He had never seen a teacher, nor ever had a teacher in school, where he saw how warmly her students responded to her. Her deep emerald eyes gleamed at them in delight at their answers and their enthusiasm to please.

And now, as he stood and delivered his homily, he'd surreptitiously check to see how pleased or otherwise she was with what he was saying. To his disappointment he never got the look she gave her pupils. But that was expected, this was not her classroom. But he longed for her, just once, a smile in approbation and appreciation, to give him even a nod that he could read as a personal interest. He would even prepare his homilies with her in mind; and at the Consecration, he'd lift the host and the chalice hoping that she would be watching his every priestly move.

He was only too happy to follow the parish priest Leo Caffrey's admonishment to pay particular attention to the First Communicants. Leo Caffrey told his curate that he made it a special point to visit the children as they prepared for their special day.

And so, Daniel O'Byrne made it his business to visit the school three times per week during religious instruction to talk to the children about the miracle that was the Sacrament of the Eucharist, that he, as their priest, had special powers to change the bread and wine into the very body and blood of Christ. He would listen to Miss Connaughton teach them about their First Confession and he helped her to line her children in front of the confessional when he brought them over to the Church to practice; and they would use ice-cream wafers and show them how to walk up reverently before the altar and open their mouths with joined prayerful hands to receive the host. He was truly impressed with the way she taught them, the way she seemed to sincerely believe in what she was doing and how she told them how important these moments were for her charges, and how it would be such an important thing in their lives to have the privilege of attending

Mass anywhere in the world, and that no matter where they were other Catholics shared their faith and belief, and that this would be a firm foundation in their lives and that, finally, as they received the final sacrament, Extreme Unction, that the Eucharistic Host would be their last meal before they died and journeyed to heaven.

All the while he stood beside her in, what he hoped was, a spiritual friendship; they were two believers in the same God, united in their love of the Church and its sacraments.

It was during this time that he made, again on the advice of Leo Caffrey, a special home visit to the parents of the communicants. This was an important visit, according to Father Leo. It was an opportunity to meet with the children's parents to advise and support them in their faith. Parents of these children, he said, were at an important time in their children's lives. If they were strong believers, it meant that their children would be loyal and dutiful members of the Church and if they were waning, or lukewarm in their faith, then all the more reason for a visit from their priest to prop them up and encourage them to be a good example to their sons and daughters. The parish priest encouraged his curate to carry some holy pictures and prayer leaflets with especial reference to the Eucharist with him on his home visits, as well as rosaries for the children making their Communion. It would be remembered and would add to the importance of their special occasion.

Chapter 9

It was Sunday afternoon. The rain had fallen all morning, but now it had cleared. Doreen's mother told them to get out of the house, 'the pair of ye, and leave me to my housework'.

Mrs Heneghan was a world-weary woman. She had a lot to be weary about, Anne thought. It was hard going for two women and a sick father to be running a farm. Anne and Doreen decided to take a cycle rather than a walk. Doreen took her father's bike while Anne was on the bike Doreen shared with her mother. They cycled out beyond the Old Mill and the Droode River and made their way into the hilly countryside out the Clochmorgan road.

They stopped at Morgan's Cross and pumped fresh cold water from the green iron pump and drank until they could take no more. Doreen had been explaining how the farm while up for sale, nothing had gone public. The Keane's and the auctioneer in Clochdroode were the only ones who knew of their plan to sell and move to Birmingham. They hoped to sell up and be in Birmingham the following spring, Easter at the latest.

"Oh, God, Doreen, I'm going to miss you so much. The place won't be the same without you."

The young women hugged and were almost in tears. "Don't, pet," Doreen rubbed Anne's back comforting her, "don't be crying. It's too hard."

They made another stop in the village of Clochmorgan, bought an ice cream and sat on a bench by the canal. The rain had held off, and patches of blue clear sky ranged over the fields beyond the canal. They were silent, listening to the birds flit and chirp around them.

Doreen sensed that Anne wanted to say something. "What's up, girl?" she asked.

Anne told her about Frankie Dalton spying on her.

"The dirty bastard, a bloody peeping-tom."

Anne sighed and cried into her hands with relief. It was so good to talk to someone who believed and understood.

Doreen put her arm around her and hugged her, "Don't let him be getting to you, Anne. He's always been odd. My mother minded him once, and she says there is something wrong with him. I think he's a spoiled brat."

Anne was taken aback, "Your mother minded him. How?"

"It's going back a bit, but Margaret Dalton asked her to help her when she was going through a bad patch."

"What do you mean?"

"I don't know the details, I was too young at the time, but seemingly after his birth Margaret got some bad turns. The doctor, you know, Doctor Travers, recommended that someone come in to help out until she got better. Doctor Travers recommended my mother. It was a way of making a bit of money. Always crying and crotchety, he was. And then a few years later, Mam was asked to take care of him a few days in the week. Margaret preferred the shop to Frankie, but at the same time spoilt him rotten; always got what he wanted.

I don't know exactly what happened, but Mam and Margaret had a falling out over how to discipline him. Frankie was getting to be too much to handle, especially as he got older and couldn't be corrected and I think he threw something at Mum, and Dad said that was the end of it. Mam told the Daltons that she couldn't look after him."

Anne could understand what Mrs Heneghan had gone through. It was much the same as what she had to go through when she was accused of hitting him. While it was somewhat reassuring to hear that Frankie was odd, maybe there was some excuse. After all, it looked like his mother wasn't much of a mother if she had to get someone else to take care of him. And it was true what Doreen said about Margaret Dalton, she much preferred to be behind the counter of the shop and bar, then be in the kitchen or nursery. But that was no consolation to Anne. She was the one who was being targeted by this spoiled brat.

"What am I going to do, Doreen?"

"Do you want to report him?"

Anne shook her head. What good would it do? It would be too embarrassing to have it out in public that she was being spied on. Anne was too private a person to want the whole of Garrydangan knowing her business.

The sun, which wasn't particularly warm became covered by a rain cloud. It grew suddenly chilly. Doreen got up and picked up her bicycle. "We'd better be heading."

They were lucky with the weather. Although there were a few drops which fell on them, the showers held off. They stopped once again at the pump at Morgan's Cross.

"You know what you could do?" Doreen said as they finished drinking the cold refreshing water. "You could take down the shed, and get the back garden cleared. That way he can't be climbing it anymore and it would be too open for him to be spying on you."

"How?"

"Tell Captain Tyrrell that it's rickety and dangerous. That it's about to fall down."

"But it isn't. It's fine."

"Ah, for God sakes girl, we'll make sure it has to come down."

"How?"

Instead of cycling directly back to Heneghans they made a stop at Anne's house. Anne followed Doreen as she made her way through the kitchen, out the back door and down the overgrown garden. The garden shed was made up of slats of wood nailed together and a tarred roof. The door hinges were stiff with rust. Anne had only been inside a few times to check it out. There was nothing in it but cobwebs, some dried-out flowers in old cracked and broken pots and a few strings of rotted onions and a rusty spade. Doreen went inside and looked around and found what she was looking for.

"Stand at the door, Anne, and hold it up as best you can."

Anne looked at her wondering what she was planning.

Doreen placed both hands on the shed and pushed as hard as she could. "Thought so. The outer section, is pretty weather beaten, it being exposed to all the rain and wind, and it's weak." She placed her two feet wide apart as if to steady herself, then she put her hands on the side wall and heaved.

There was a loud crack.

"Jesus, Doreen, be careful."

Doreen ignored her. After the first heave, she could feel the give she was looking for. She told Anne to walk away from the door on the outside. She gave another heave and as she felt the nails give way and heard a creaking, she gave one last heave and ran out the door. There was another creak and the roof caved in a few inches and then the shed steadied again, but it was now lob-sided, and looked as if it could fall down at any moment.

Doreen stood back to check her handiwork.

"That'll do the job."

Anne laughed, "You're a mad one, girl."

"Maybe, but there's method in it," she snorted a grin and rubbed Anne's shoulder in triumph. "Now it's ready for Captain Tyrrell to inspect."

The following day, after school, Anne went directly to the Gate Lodge Office. Hubert Tyrrell was on the phone, but as soon as he saw Anne he smiled and indicated that he was finishing his conversation. He put the phone on its cradle and smiled again, "Well, Miss Connaughton, what can I do for you?"

Anne was struck by the smile. It was unusually warm and ready to listen. "I'm worried about the garden shed, Captain."

"Call me Hubert, Miss Connaughton, I prefer Hubert."

"Well, Hubert, the shed is about to collapse and I'm wondering could you arrange to have it taken down."

"I didn't realise there was one, but I suppose there must be," he said jauntily, "I tell you what, I'll call over there in about an hour when I close the office. Is that ok? And I'll take a look."

Anne wasn't expecting he would do something about it so soon. "If it's not too inconvenient."

He stood up from the table and came over to her, "No, not at all." He was about to say more but decided not to. "I'll see you in about an hour."

Anne was in the kitchen drinking tea when she heard a knock. It was Captain Tyrrell. She was surprised to see him, thought that he was merely fobbing her off; that he would send one of the workers to attend to the shed.

"May I come in?"

"Of course." Anne directed him to the back door which led to the garden.

He shook his head when he saw the garden. "This place is a bit of a mess, isn't it?" he wasn't expecting an answer, "must get it sorted out."

He made his way to the shed, Anne followed him.

"Yes, I see what you mean. It could fall at any moment." He took off his jacket. "Would you mind?"

She held the jacket. Then he handed her his waistcoat and tie. "You can take those inside, I'll be in in a jiffy."

Anne walked back to the house. She was impressed with his energy and was not a little flushed in the face. He was more handsome than she first thought. His hands were working hands, not soft, office hands. She placed his clothes on the back of the chair and watched him as he worked. He knew what he was doing. Within a few minutes, he had cleared the shed and somehow had found a hammer and crowbar and went about totally demolishing it.

He came into the house sweating and looking pleased with himself. "That felt good," he said. "I'll get Tommy to clear it out and to do a bit of work on the garden for you. If that's okay with you?"

Anne nodded her thanks and offered him tea and biscuits.

He agreed with alacrity. They sat down. He asked about her, where she was from. She told him. She was surprised at how easy it was to talk to him about herself, but she wasn't shy of asking him about himself. To which he seemed easy and happy to do so.

It was getting dark when he checked his watch, "Must get going." He stood to put on his tie, waistcoat and jacket.

Anne walked him to the door. Before they reached the front door, he turned to her, and looked at her shyly.

"I hope you don't think me impertinent, Miss Connaughton, but I have two tickets for the Abbey."

"Oh," Anne didn't know what he meant. Did he mean that he had two tickets to give her if she wanted to take a friend, or was he actually asking her out? "I don't know, Captain, I mean, Hubert."

"I apologise if I am being a little forward, Miss Connaughton, but I have two tickets for next week. It's one of Lennox Robinson's. *Drama at Inish,* a comedy, I think. I was wondering, you know, if you were able to, I mean, if you had the time."

Anne blushed at realising that he was asking her out. It was the last thing she expected and was hesitant. But he seemed to be genuine and he was smiling at her in hope. It would be bad manners to refuse. She nodded, for she couldn't bring herself to speak for fear she would make a fool of herself.

"Okay, then. I'll pick you up next Tuesday."

Suddenly the implications of her agreeing to go overcame her. "Well, er, I don't know."

"Is there a problem?"

"Well, Hubert," she looked at him more confidently now, "I am delighted that you have asked me, but I'd prefer you didn't pick me up. It would be better to meet somewhere, er…"

He nodded, "Of course," he smiled with relief. "I understand completely. The wagging tongues of Garrydangan, and all that. Well, then what do you propose?"

She thought for a moment. "I have a friend who works in Clochdroode, in McElroys. I'll meet you there."

He bowed to her and smiled. "McElroys it is, so."

Chapter 10

Father O'Byrne left the Delamere's and got into his black Morris Minor and made his way to the Keanes.

He was very happy with his visit to the Delamere's. He was treated very deferentially, tea was offered in the best china with Oxford Lunch fruitcake served on Mrs Delamere's best china, and linen serviettes. He met with young Charles, the First Communicant, gave the child his rosary and Holy picture, which delighted Mrs Delamere. 'Most unexpected, and most welcome, Father'. He was asked to bless the rosary beads, holy card and the young man as well as the family. He left feeling that his priestly duties were fulfilled and his position as a priest was appreciated by his flock.

Father O'Byrne had never been to the Keane household. When he drove up to the front gate, he was pleasantly surprised at how neat the garden was with roses and trimmed neat hedges. He was welcomed by Mrs Keane into a small, tidy kitchen.

"You are most welcome, Father. I'm sorry the place is in a mess, but you can sit there beside the Stanley and keep yourself warm."

Father O'Byrne sat down and noticed the Sacred Heart picture hanging on the wall complete with red votive lamp. A rosary beads was hanging from it.

A little girl was standing smiling at him as he sat. He wasn't used to children and didn't quite know how to speak to her.

"Antoinette, go out to Dad and tell him the priest, Father O'Byrne, is here."

The little girl smiled at the priest and ran out.

"I wasn't expecting you, Father, sure, aren't you great to pay us a visit."

"I'm sorry if I came at a bad time."

"Not at all, not at all, it's just that if I had known I would have made a currant cake."

"Now, don't be bothering, Mrs Keane, a cup of tea would be fine."

Sylvia Keane was a slim handsome woman, of quick decisive movements. She had the kettle on the Stanley already boiling and reached up to the top of the press to get the good teapot and the best cups and saucers she kept back for important occasions.

"Nice place you have here, Mrs Keane, lovely roses."

"Ah, sure they're not the best, Father, the weather is not great for them this year."

Antoinette came back, "Da says he'll be in the soonest."

Father O'Byrne looked at the child, "Is this the girl that's making her Communion?"

"Yes, Father," the girl answered shyly.

"And what's your name?"

"Antoinette, Father. And I'm seven years old."

She was like an angel. Her blond hair and pretty smile radiated goodness and innocence.

"Now, girl, don't be standing there, give me a hand with the cups and saucers."

Antoinette smiled with delight. She was going to be setting the good cups and saucers, and because the priest was here there was going to be the cake Mam had bought for Sunday and biscuits as well.

"I have something, for you Antoinette," the priest took out a small white leather purse and a Holy picture.

Antoinette's eye's widened with unexpected delight. "Look, Mam, look what I got?"

"Ah, sure you shouldn't have, Father."

The little girl showed her mother the white beads and card. Her face was beaming. Father O'Byrne felt his heart skip. It was pure pleasure to him to see how a small token could mean so much to this little girl. He too was smiling and unconsciously beaming in a similar manner to Antoinette.

"Can I show Father O'Byrne my altar, Mam."

"Now, now, don't be bothering the poor man. I'm sure he's too busy to be looking at your altar."

The pain and disappointment on the little girl's face was too much to bear. "Of course, I'd love to see your altar."

She looked pleadingly at her mother, who smiled indulgently, "Okay, just this once."

Antoinette had already had her hands in his and was leading the priest to her bedroom. "It's in here, Father."

Father O'Byrne was pleased at how guileless she was and how pure and innocently she, with his hands in hers, was brought into her room.

"There it is, Father." She pointed to the corner.

The bedroom was tiny, but it was neat and clean, and the altar was a small wooden box on which a statue of Our Lady stood with a vase of flowers and an unlit candle beside the statue.

"I light the candle at night just before I go to bed, I say my prayers and then I blow it out. Mammy lets me," she said proudly.

Mrs Keane was at the bedroom door. "Come on now, Antoinette, let Father O'Byrne come in and have his tea."

"But he has to say a prayer first." The little girl said as if it were the most normal thing in the world for a priest to do in front of a stature of Our Lady.

Father O'Byrne smiled indulgently and took out his purple Stole, kissed it reverently, and placed it around his neck. Antoinette was awed at the ritual and she knelt down in front of her altar as she would do each night. Father O'Byrne knelt beside her, they recited the Our Father, the Hail Mary and the Glory be together. Father O'Byrne then stood up and blessed the altar. Antoinette remained kneeling. Mrs Keane could see how much this meant to her daughter. She wiped a tear and blessed herself.

"Come on now and help me serve the tea."

Tomás Keane came in just as the tea was being poured.

"Come in Tomás now, and have a cup of tea," Mrs Keane told him as he took his cap off and hung it on a nail behind the door.

"Father," he nodded to the priest in greeting and sat at the table.

"Look at what Father gave me, Dad." Antoinette proudly showed her father the white rosary beads and holy picture.

Mr Keane took them in his hand and showed excitement, "Isn't that very good of him, now."

"It's for her Communion, Mr Keane," Father O'Byrne explained, "I'm visiting the families of those who are receiving their First Holy Communion." He detected a note of criticism, or at least, reluctance to be beholden to this priest.

"That's okay, Father. You needn't be explaining. I appreciate the gesture."

"Now, Tomás," Mrs Keane, handed him a side plate with a slice of cake, "put that beside you and drink up your tea."

Tomás looked at her and shook his head. Father O'Byrne realised that he was being told to behave himself in front of the priest.

"Isn't it grand weather out there, now, thank God," Mrs Keane said as she sat at the table.

"It is indeed," the priest said, sensing the tension in the kitchen, and that he was its source.

Antoinette sat with them eating her cake and telling the priest about how many animals they had and the number of eggs the chickens were laying.

"That was an interesting sermon you gave last week, Father."

"Oh, yes?" The priest said, not sure whether he was being praised or criticised.

Mrs Keane looked at her husband as if to check him. But he wasn't going to heed.

"Yes, about what happened on Pattern Day."

Mrs Keane, who saw that Antoinette had finished her cake and her tea, said, "Now, Antoinette, you go out there and play for a while, and make sure you thank Father O'Byrne for his lovely gift."

Antoinette was reluctant to leave, she wanted to be with the adults when they were talking but knew her mother was not going to allow her on this occasion, for reasons she could not fathom. She got up from her chair and smiled at the priest and thanked him for the rosary beads.

"You seem to be blaming us for what happened." Tomás Keane said, leaning forward in the chair.

"Now Tomás, I'm sure it wasn't that way at all," Mrs Keane stood and gathered the side plates. "Would you like more tea, Father?"

"Give the man more tea, Sylvia." Keane said to her.

"Yes, I'll have another cup, if you don't mind."

"You don't know much about us, Father, do you?"

The priest looked at Mrs Keane who was now at the sink, deliberately ignoring her husband.

"I'm not sure what you mean, Mr Keane."

"Do you know where we're from?"

"What do you mean?"

"We're Mayo people, Father."

"Yes, I know that."

"But do you know what part. Do you know why we had to come here?"

The priest was silent. He felt a note of resentment but could not figure where it originated.

"We're from Erris, Father. And if you don't know Erris, then I can tell you that it's the most God forsaken part of the country you could ever lay eyes on. I, we, weren't born here. Except for Antoinette. She's the only one born here. The rest of the family are Mayo people, Michael the oldest and young Tommy. We came here about ten years ago. We only had twenty acres, Father, twenty acres of rock, bog, and water.

You couldn't make a living out of it. But we were offered this place. Forty acres, plus ten of bog for turf, a house and a shed. That was it. We came here and we worked hard, didn't we, Sylvia?"

Mrs Keane remained at the sink not wanting to be dragged into the discussion.

"My people, I mean, me father and mother had a tough life. I don't know how they managed. My aunt and uncle were lost on the Titanic when it went down. On their way to America like so many before them and more after. The place was haemorrhaging people, Father. There was nothing worth staying for. The whole of the west of Ireland from Donegal, to Mayo, to Galway and down to Kerry was the same. The Congested Districts they called it, Father. Too many people, not enough land. What else was there but poverty, the boat to America, or England or even Australia? I have two older brothers and a sister in Boston. One has moved on out to Chicago. What else was there to do? We have lost our best people."

"I'm sure Father O'Byrne is aware of all that, Tomás."

Father O'Byrne nodded, "I know what you mean, Mr Keane."

"You are an educated man, Father. I know you know your history. The famine, the Land League. The great work Davitt did and Parnell. I'm sure you know all that. But do you know us, I mean, do you know your parishioners, and what we had to go through, and what we still have to go through?"

"Now, Tomás, I'm sure Father…"

"But he hasn't a clue, Sylvia. That's what I'm saying, and your sermon there last week demonstrated to me, and to a lot of people your ignorance Father."

Daniel O'Byrne had never been spoken to in the way he was being spoken to now; he had never once in his life been criticised for any sermon he had ever delivered. He could feel anger at the impertinence that was being demonstrated by this farmer. He was about to say that he was a priest of God and that no one had the right to criticise him. Not him personally, but he, as God's anointed and His representative here on earth. But he couldn't find the words. They seemed to constrict at his throat.

"We came here, Father, and I mean the Heneghans, the Kneafseys, the MacDonaghs, the Ruanes from the west of Ireland, not because we wanted to, but because we had no other choice. Do you think that any of us wanted to leave our land and our native county? Do you think any of us would leave what was familiar to us and come here to an alien place, to a people that hates us and resents us?"

"Now, Tomás, not everyone is like that." His wife was now facing him at the sink, "You go on a bit too much about that."

"I know. I know, Sylvia." Her husband relented, "Of course there are people here who accept us and are happy with us being here, and they are good, decent people. But you know as well as I that there are others who are very different, very different. And you know them, and I know them."

"Now, now, Tomás."

"I won't, Sylvia. This man needs to know the truth about what is going on here, in his own parish. I have no objection to most of the farmers here, I mean the families who have had their farms from the time of Davitt and the Land League and even those before that. But what gets my goat is the shower who wouldn't raise their fingers to work their own land; are too bloody lazy and want hand-outs and make excuses, or are afraid to take risks to buy a farm, or put into the Land Commission for a farm, and bloody well work it and make a success of it. Those are the very ones who start fights and create trouble in these parts, marching with posters and writing to politicians, and rioting in the streets of Clochdroode, saying that there are too many blow-ins in the town, taking their land. Their land! Too fucken lazy to work the land themselves, but they tell us we are taking their bloody land! Do you know what they call us, Father, do you know?"

Father O'Byrne shook his head, not that he didn't know what they were called, but he didn't know what to say.

"Migrants! Migrants they call us, as if we were tinkers. That's what they think of us, Father, less than tinkers!"

Antoinette came to the back door, "Mam I need a basket for the eggs."

"That's enough, now, Tomás," Mrs Keane said as she wiped her hand on the towel and reached up for the basket and handed it to her daughter, "be careful with them, now, lass, don't break any."

Antoinette went away excited. She was rarely allowed to collect and carry the eggs by herself.

Tomás Keane relented, "Look, Father, I'm sorry if I have offended you or hurt your feelings. But you need to know the real reason for what happened on Pattern Day."

Father O'Byrne had known most of what Tomás Keane had told him but he had to admit that he didn't realise the depth of feeling, or how so near the surface it was. Given what he heard it wasn't surprising that there was a flare up. All it took was a spark.

"It doesn't take too much in these parts, Father," Sylvia said as she sat down at the table. "There's an undercurrent of anger and resentment that gets surfaced, if you know what I mean, at times."

"No, I see what you mean, Mrs Keane. I wasn't aware of the depth of it."

"And that's what's behind that Dalton bastard and his killing of my sheep."

"I'm not sure I understand you."

"You can't be saying that, Tomás." Sylvia Keane shook her head, "That young lad is sick. He's not well."

"Sick my arse," Keane made no effort to apologise for his language in front of the priest, and he let his wife know by a look and gesture that he didn't care. "He wouldn't kill a sheep belonging to the Egans or Geoghans, would he? Knows what would bloody well happen to him, he would. Get the shite kicked out of him. Lucky we only killed his bloody dog."

The priest was shocked at what he had just heard. Mrs Keane shook her head annoyed at her husband for mentioning the incident. God only knew what would happen now.

"It's the truth, Sylvia, and I'm not afraid of admitting it. Eye for an eye. Ain't I right, Father?"

"I'm not sure I'd agree in this case, Mr Keane."

"There's justice, Father. Even the Bible says so. 'Eye for an eye, tooth for a tooth', Father."

"I'm not sure that that was…"

"You can't be having a loose dog around farms with animals unless they are under a leash or are able to be made behave themselves. Can you? You can't. And that bloody bastard let his dog loose on our sheep."

"We don't know that." his wife said, "There's no proof."

"Proof? What proof do you need, woman? That dog was never seen wandering around the village or around the place on his own. He's either stuck by the shop or he is with that mad bastard of a son, Frankie Dalton. That guy is touched, Father. He needs, what do you call it? You know when there is a devil inside you?"

"Exorcism."

"Ah, come on, Tomás, that's going a bit far."

"Not a bit of it, Sylvia. That fella will land himself in trouble one of these days."

Antoinette came back carrying the basket, "Look, I found four eggs!" She was proud of herself and came over to show her father and the priest.

"Aren't you the topper," her father said as he ruffled her head gently.

The priest looked at the eggs and the little girl with pleasure. They were a good family, a good Catholic family. They had a hard life and they didn't complain except for the injustices they saw and experienced. But little Antoinette was their hope and his hope also. It would be her generation that would heal the resentments and the blind, tribal, hatred that was a cancer within the parish. A child would save them. Wasn't that His promise? The Lion would lie down with the Lamb. There was hope. He believed that. God would see to it.

Chapter 11

"Well, come on, girl, tell us!" Doreen was a bundle of excitement.

"There's nothing to tell."

Both women met, as arranged, at the foot of the road leading to the Heneghan and Keane farms.

"Well, what did ye do, what's he like, then? You can at least tell me that." Doreen linked Anne's arm as they walked the boreen by the quarry.

Anne told her about how he picked her up outside, or behind, McElroys and drove up to Dublin. The play was great fun. They went to a pub afterwards and then he drove Anne back home.

"Straight home?"

"Of course! What did you think?"

"Och, sure I don't know, I've never been out with a Protestant Englishman." Doreen laughed, and turned to Anne, "Are you sure he didn't do anything."

"What do you mean, 'do anything'? What do you take me for?"

"So, what yer sayin' is that he was the gentleman."

Anne smiled at the way Doreen said 'gentleman', as if she were describing a Hollywood Matinee idol. "Yes," she mimicked Doreen, "he was a gentleman."

"And you are saying he never tried anything."

"No, Doreen," Anne tugged Doreen's arm, and laughed, "I'd say there was a bit of North of Ireland Presbyterian in him."

"Ah, jays, God help you so."

Both women laughed. They continued to walk arm in arm. The honeysuckle was in blossom and the blackbirds whistled and ruffled the hedges.

And that is what he was, Anne thought as they passed the quarry and made a turn towards the Heneghan farm, a Protestant gentleman. There was no North of Ireland Presbyterian in him, as he said himself, he was Anglo, with a dash of native Irish stock.

Anne told Doreen as much as she herself knew about Captain Hubert Tyrrell. He was the nephew of Lady Tyrrell, who had married into the Anglo-Irish Tyrrells of the Baronies of Clochdroode and Garrydangan. In fact, Hubert's uncle, Charles, was his mother's younger brother. Sir Charles and Lady Constance were childless, and Hubert was the only surviving child of the Tyrrell family.

"But what about Hubert's mother? What happened to her?" Doreen asked.

"From what I can gather, she did not marry well."

"How romantic!" Doreen sighed, "Did she fall in love with the gardener, or gamekeeper, or something? That'd be a great picture to go to."

"No, not the gardener, nor gamekeeper, but the Major in Athlone Barracks. Hence, the Army influence. He, Hubert, had huge admiration for his father who fought with the Leinster Regiment in Ypres and the Somme. Came back to Athlone and retired there. He died some years back. Not sure how or under what circumstances."

"And his mother, what about her?"

"He didn't say a whole lot about her. Not sure if that was because we didn't have time or whether it was because we spent more time talking about his father and the army. Hubert, like his father joined the army, but not the Irish Army. Why? He said that his father told him that if he wanted a career in the Army, he'd do better in England. That in a post-Independent Ireland no Anglo-Irish Protestant gentleman, of the Landlord class was going to get anywhere. And that's what he did and he ended up in India. The 'great adventure' as he called it."

Doreen didn't ask any more questions. Anne was thankful for her tact. It wasn't the time or place to get into the too personal, and the as yet, unknown regions of a relationship that had only started by a chance meeting and a random request to accompany a gentleman to the theatre.

But where would it lead? He was a Protestant. She a Catholic. Already there were impediments. But religious belief wasn't the only possible difficulty. There was class, social status. He was, obviously, Gentry, Anglo-Irish gentry. A different culture, a different way of looking and living out one's life. He was army. That was not necessarily an obstacle, but it had shaped him and influenced his ways. He was reticent, stiff, not arrogant, or haughty, but he knew his position, or his place in society, and this gave him a confidence and a well-defined identity. She wasn't sure how much he could bend or soften. He was handsome, in a manly, product-of-the-male-world sort of way; his body was lithe and strong, his smile, when he allowed himself to smile, was warm and respectful, and she hoped, and was confident, would be loving, or, could be.

He was, as she described to Doreen, a gentleman. There was no hint of him taking advantage of her in any way. He did not even suggest that they stay overnight somewhere, either in his house, which was in Drumcondra, or in a hotel, grubby or up-market, and which he could have felt he had the chance to offer, or suggest, something else, but that something else would not be what Anne would have wanted. And he seemed, at least seemed, to divine that that was not where she was; and that was a relief.

He was, indeed, a gentleman. There was no effort, by either word or gesture that they hold hands while walking to and from the theatre. There was no effort on his part, while in conversation in the pub, that he felt he had the right, or opportunity, to sit too close, or touch hands; and on their return journey and, especially when he pulled in to McElroys to pick up her bike, and subsequently to drop her off at the crossroads outside Garrydangan, so that they would not be seen together, he did not try to kiss her, or request any intimacy beyond a polite goodnight, and a promised hope to see her again.

While there was no question that she enjoyed his company, and that he seemed to enjoy hers, there was no plan, or hint of a plan, to meet again. In fact, while Anne would have desired another 'date' or another chance to meet with him socially, she wasn't at all sure that he had a similar desire.

All this she could not tell Doreen, but she was confident that Doreen understood; that she would respect Anne's confidence and would, in time, in the manner that women friends knew these things, would be privy to them when the appropriate time arose.

The following Tuesday Anne awoke to noises in the back garden. She checked the back window. She recognised workmen from Tyrrell House talking among themselves and carrying shovels, pickaxes and crowbars. She dressed and went down to them.

Tommie Lawless, the head gardener, saluted her, "Mornin' Miss. Sorry for disturbin' you this early in the mornin', but the Captain says we had to get to it as soon as possible."

"And what's that, Mr Lawless?"

"Sure, we've to fix up this mess of a garden, Miss. Get rid of that old bockety shed."

Anne was delighted. "That's great, Mr Lawless. Thanks very much."

"Sure, don't be thankin' us, Miss. It's himself gives the orders."

A warm glow flowed through her. This was really very good of him. "Are you alright for everything? Would ye like tea or anything?"

"We're only after the breakfast. Sure if you leave the kitchen open so we can boil some water later on we'd appreciate it."

Anne waved at them, "That's no bother."

By the time Anne got back from school, the workmen had departed. The garden was cleared, the grass mowed, and the shed was gone. The wild hedge at the back was trimmed down and a flowerbed was dug out and bounded by rocks placed neatly to form a low wall. What delighted her most was the view she had. She could now sit in the garden and look out and had a clear view of the sloping fields that stretched out beyond Garrydangan. And there was another advantage, which was a secret relief, there was no way Frankie Dalton would be able to sneak in and spy on her. It was far too open for him. There was no place for him to hide.

On the following morning, Anne woke up with the joyful anticipation of opening her curtains and seeing the garden in its morning glory. At first, the smile of delight and joy overwhelmed her. The garden almost sparkled in the morning sun.

Her eyes caught something in the newly trimmed back hedge at the far corner of the garden.

"Oh, God," she fell back onto her bed; she covered her face and was overcome with tears. She tried to wipe away the image of what she had seen. A dead cat lying stretched out in full length across the hedge.

Chapter 12

"That bitch is at it again. Blaming my son in the wrong!"

"The Captain saw it, Margaret, on the hedge. It's his property. The dead cat was on his property."

"But it was her that blamed Frankie. No one else. She has it in for him. Always had."

Frank and Margaret Dalton were in the kitchen finishing their supper after they closed for the night.

"And why would he be coming to you and telling you? You know why, the pair of them are great with one another. Oh, Josie Fagan has seen and heard things. Coming in late at night and the two of them meeting out the road, as if no one would see them. Hah! She has him wrapped around her little finger. Mark my words, Frank, I'm telling you, she'll be Mrs Tyrrell, soon enough, bloody Lady of the Manor. And where will your plans be then, eh?"

Dalton shivered as he heard his wife tell him what he had been fearing. But he was in business long enough to know that not everything worked out as planned. What he knew, and what his wife did not know, was that the Captain had no interest in running the manor or anything to do with the land. The Captain was a city gent. He had no real fears of Miss Connaughton spoiling his plans. If, as Josie Fagan was implying, and Frank always took what Josie said with a large pinch of salt, Anne Connaughton would move to Dublin, live high and mighty in Rathmines after Lady Constance had passed away. He, Dalton, still had his dreams and they were of the type that could be a reality. Let Hubert Tyrrell marry whomever he willed, or not marry, if he so chooses, but he, Frank Dalton, would be Lord of the Manor. In his own time, in his own way.

Dalton didn't tell his wife the rest of what he heard about his son. The Captain had come into the bar, as was his usual habit on Fridays and, of course, both men got into the usual conversation about business and their plans. Then the Captain mentioned the dead cat. He told Dalton that he'd been talking to Miss Connaughton who had complained to him, as her landlord, that she had seen Frankie spying on her one night. And that that had led to him having to clean up the place and knock down a perfectly good shed and get rid of a very necessary hedge which acted as a perfect property boundary. That this, now trimmed back boundary hedge, was where the dead cat was placed. And, as Dalton had further inquired as to the link with his son, he was informed that it was the opinion of the Captain that it indeed was Frankie, that, in the Captain's opinion, it was his son's way of getting back at her for preventing him from spying on her again and in the future.

Of course, he had to accept the veracity of what he had been told by the Captain, and it was something he could never mention to his wife. There was the reality that he knew, or accepted, that his son was odd, or at least troublesome. That this was a result of his mother having a bad time of it during the birth, and of not being able to nurse him or take care of him properly for quite a while, and this led to guilt on the part of his mother who, subsequently compensated by spoiling him and giving in to him hither and thither.

There was another reality which Dalton had to factor into his thinking. He could not be seen to be too critical of the Captain, or be seen by him, the Captain, as not taking his opinion of his son seriously, because it was obvious that the Captain accepted Miss Connaughton's version of events. If he had no business relationship with the Captain, he could dismiss what he had been told about his son, and reminded the Captain that it was all hearsay, that Miss Connaughton had a history of antipathy towards his son. But he needed to keep the Captain on board with regard to his and John Holton's plans. The Captain was a necessary piece of the jigsaw, an integral part of the foundation of his and their fortune.

But, even if that were not the case, in his heart of hearts, Dalton knew that what he had been told of his son was true, or if not true, at least was very likely something he would and could do.

So, what was he to do? The summer holidays weren't too far ahead. He couldn't have Frankie hanging around Garrydangan all summer. God knows what he'd get himself up to.

By chance, as the conversation with the Captain, twisted and turned, Dalton, almost pleading, asked the Captain, "What should I do? He's a handful. I'll tell you that."

"How old is he?" the Captain asked.

"Sixteen."

The Captain took a sip from his whiskey and thought for a moment. "I'm an army man, Mr Dalton, young fellas like him should be active, should have no time to be thinking of any mischief, should be so busy that at night the only thing they want or desire is to go to bed; and they need to be worked so hard, that that is all they think of, work, sleep, and of course, good feeding."

"You're right, Captain. But he's too young for the army."

"Well, do you know anyone that will work him to exhaustion?"

"That's it." Dalton tapped the counter, "Granny Mills."

"Who?"

"He always loved his granny. Margaret's mother. She had a way with him. There was no messing with her. He was like putty in her hands. That's what I'll do. He can spend the summer with his granny and his uncles on the farm. There's plenty of cows to be milked, hay to be saved and turf turned and brought home."

He put this to his wife. She agreed. It would get him out of Garrydangan and the area for a while. He'd be off her hands. He'd be happy with her mother. She'd put manners on him, and by the end of the summer he'd be ready to go back to the Jesuits in Tullybeg. Get him an education, maybe even go to Trinity, or Earlsfort Terrace; do what his father wanted him to do, become a businessman. Do a degree in business, come back to Garrydangan and make her proud. He'd be a Dalton of Garrydangan and in time, owner of Tyrrell House. There would be no end to his ambition; he'd marry well, she'd make sure of that; she'd have grandchildren to console her in her old age. Yes, he had outgrown Garrydangan. Her mother would whip him into shape. The Jesuits would make a man of him. The future was bright.

Chapter 13

Granny Mills said he was a great worker. That he had the makings of a real farmer. It was great being with Granny Mills. When he brought in the cows and tied them up in the shed, Granny said that it was marvellous how the cows did what they were told that he had a great way with them. And then when he and his uncle were finished milking the cows, well, it was mostly his uncle who actually did the milking, but his uncle said he'd teach him how to do it, Granny had a great feed for them. Bacon, cabbage, plenty of spuds and always, after he had finished it all up she'd have made a rhubarb tart, or a baked apple cake with lashings of Birds Custard. He loved his granny's cooking. It was much better than his mothers. Mam hardly ever baked a pie or a cake. It was always a bought cake. He much preferred a real freshly cooked out of the oven cake, as well as soda bread and he couldn't have enough of her brown bread.

But the work he loved most was saving the hay. After the hay was cut, it had to be rowed, and then turned to dry in the sun. He loved handling the hayfork and walking to one side of his uncle and turning it. There were some days when they'd have help from one of the neighbours, the Kirwans, who would help with the making of the cocks. He loved gathering the final fork of hay and topping the cock, giving it a good slap and his uncle, or Mr Kirwan say, "That's it, lad, give it a good slap to steady it." And they would move on to make the next cock. And after a while it got so easy. He had muscles he never thought he had, so his granny said with admiration. Mr Kirwan said he was a topper with the hay. A natural, his uncle said. And then it was out to the fields to get the cows and bring them into the shed and tie them up and he even got to milk a few. Although it wasn't as easy as he thought. It annoyed him that he couldn't do it as well or as quick as his uncle, but Granny Mills said, "Sure, you can't be good at everything and sure it takes a born farmer years to perfect the knack."

But then to top it all, he saw Phyllis Kirwan one day, coming out to the men in the field with plates full of sandwiches and tea. It was when they were giving the Kirwans a couple of days to help them save their hay. That was the best few days he ever spent. Phyllis was older than him, she was eighteen, and she was the best looking girl in Cadamstown, according to his uncle, who he could see liked her a lot, but he was too old, and anyway he was going out with Katie Dunne from over in Knockcavan. But he agreed with his uncle, Phyllis Kirwan was the best-looking girl for miles around and she was the girl he'd love to be able to go out with.

At first, Phyllis didn't notice him. She came out with the sandwiches and tea, poured out the tea and milk, asked if there was anything else they wanted. He knew what he wanted, but he knew she wouldn't give it to him. He tried to catch her eye but she wouldn't give him the satisfaction. But he was sure that she was just being shy, or playing shy among the men, that she was afraid of her father and brothers, who were older than her. And then on the second day after the sandwiches were eaten he managed to make an excuse to go to the toilet. It was when he was in the house that he saw her over the sink washing the dishes. He could feel the excitement of seeing her leaning over the sink, her arms were bare as she washed the dishes, her body moving as she took the plates out and placed them on the drain and what was best of all was the smile she gave him. It was almost too much for him. He had to hide the hardness in his trousers. She looked at him and smiled again. He went red with embarrassment. But he liked the smile and the look she gave him. By the time he went to the bathroom, he was so hard he had to rub his mickey and yank it so that he could feel the explosion and get relief. He wiped himself with the toilet paper and was more relaxed when he went back into the kitchen again. He looked at her with more confidence now. He knew he was big for his age, and what with all the farming he'd been doing he knew that he was getting bigger and bigger by the day. His granny said so. He was really proud of himself when he caught her eye and nodded to her and said, "See ya," as he left.

And then to top it all he was allowed to go to the dance in Cadamstown Parish Hall on the Saturday night. He was allowed to cycle to the dance and come home by himself. He put his bike up against the wall and went in. There weren't that many in the hall. There were a few girls sitting on one side talking and giggling, and a few lads on the other side leaning against the wall watching everyone as they came in. He went over to the lads. They knew him through his granny and uncle and they chatted about where he was from and what school he went to. When he told them that he went to Tullybeg, they shook their heads, but he made sure that they didn't think him a big shot or a snob. He talked like they talked and asked who the women were across the room. They made jokes about them and he felt better, he was just like them. Then later, at about ten o'clock he saw her coming in with a group of lads. They were laughing and talking out loud. They were drunk, or at least they had been drinking a lot. He couldn't tell if Phyllis had been drinking but he didn't care as long as he was able to dance with her. He couldn't take his eyes off her, and even the lads noticed. They said she was Phyllis the 'filly' and she was a ride. He didn't like the way they talked about her and he let them know by the way he looked at them that he was not going to let them away with it. But all that did not matter, what mattered was that he caught her looking at him and when she did he felt the excitement go through his body. He smiled back and was about to go over to ask her to dance when one of the lads she came in with pulled her out onto the floor. But he would make sure he got his chance. He watched how the other lads went over to the other side of the hall and how they managed to get a girl out to dance. Most of the girls were happy to be asked and they smiled, looked at one another shyly and giggled and that's when they knew that she was interested. He watched one particular lad who went over to a really pretty girl, she was obviously a Convent girl, one of the goody-goodies, as the lads said. But this lad went over and kind of bowed his head and put out his hand. All he had to do was nod at her and she smiled and bowed back and walked with him onto the floor. It was a waltz and he watched them as they seemed to glide all over the floor. He thought he could do that, that all he had to do was kind of walk to the music. He'd try it with Phyllis when she was finished with the fella she was dancing with now.

But after that dance she didn't go back with him. She went outside by herself. He was wondering was he imagining it when he thought that she glanced at him as she left. Then all of a sudden he was outside the hall. The music playing inside. People were coming in and out, smoking and talking and the giggling going on in places he couldn't see. It was real dark now.

He heard his name. It was her. She was standing across the road. She was smoking. She was by herself. He went over to her. She took him by the hand and led him down the road to where there was a wall. He couldn't say a word, he didn't know what to say. All he knew was that he wanted to be with her and wanted to do something to her that he had never done with a girl before. But he didn't know what that was. Then in the dark with her back to the wall she pulled him into her and the hardness of his mickey was so quick he couldn't help but rub it up against her. And as he did she pulled him into her and started rubbing herself off him as well. It was the best feeling he had ever had in his life. She was kissing him and then she was sucking on his tongue. At first, he pulled away but she said it was alright, not to worry. And he liked that too. And then she was breathing heavily against him and he was so hard he couldn't take it anymore and his body wanted to explode, or at least that part of his body did and then they pulled one another tightly and held one another until the excitement went away. And then she kissed him called him a good boy and she walked back to the hall. He didn't know what to do. Should he follow her? Is that what she wanted? But she didn't look back. And then as he turned to make his way back to the hall he couldn't believe how cold it was down there. He was wet. He became frightened, he thought he had pissed on himself. He checked. It was only a spot in the front. He realised it was the white stuff, the same white stuff that came out when he exploded with the excitement. It was like a safety valve in a steam engine. His uncle told him that there had to be a safety valve in a steam engine otherwise the engine would explode. That explained the feeling he had when his mickey got hard and became so hard he almost exploded. That made sense. He couldn't go back to the hall and he all wet. He would stay outside and hope it would dry off.

He took out the packet of cigarettes his uncle gave him before he left for the dance. "You'll might be needing these," he said. He wondered did his uncle do the same with Katie Dunne. But he wasn't going to be asking him. He walked back to the hall but did not go in. He stood at the door checking to see if his trousers had dried. But he wasn't too bothered to go in anyway. After what they did together, dancing was a poor thing to be doing with a girl. He looked around to see Phyllis. She was talking to some girl and two lads. But she didn't look back at him or didn't look around to see if he was back in the hall. She just was there leaning up against the wall; they might as well be talking about the weather, or farming. There was no point going back in. He'd wait for a while to see if she came out looking for him. But she didn't. But that didn't matter. He'd see her again, this time he would be sure to be by himself with her with no distractions and no other lads taking away her attention.

A chance came. All the hay was in. There would be no more work to be done on that. He had finished helping his uncle with the milking. There was nothing else to do. The evening was dry and warm. He was bored and needed to get out of the house. He had no interest in talking with adults about local gossip, and who married who years ago, and how many children they had now, and what land was up for sale and might be worth a look at; neither was he a bit interested in politics and what DeValera was going to do now that the election was lost, thanks be to God, and how they hoped they wouldn't see hide not hair of him from now on; or what the parish priest said off the pulpit about what was on the radio and giving out about all the new-fangled music that was being heard and not our own beautiful Irish music. And how the world was going to hell in a hand basket. He had been listening to the same conversations all summer. He'd take his bike out and ride around the town land, get rid of the boredom.

He knew where he wanted to go. Had been doing it on and off when he got the chance. He rode around behind the Kirwans and hid his bike in a ditch. There was a great spot he found where he could look into Phyllis's bedroom. He'd watch her walking around her room and he'd get the excitement. He was lucky to catch her once taking off her clothes. That was the best night. His mickey was exploding but he found a way to keep the excitement going until he couldn't hold it in anymore, by taking his mickey in his and rubbing it in a similar way to the way she did it to him, and he kept rubbing and pulling it until he had to let go and then he was careful to make sure he didn't wet his trousers and when he was done he wiped his hands in the grass.

But tonight he was going to do something he hadn't tried before. He would knock on her window and hope she'd let him in. He waited until she was about to take off her clothes. He crouched low behind the ditch and then slowly like a cowboy making sure no one was watching he made his way to her window. He tapped on it. There was no response. He tapped on it this time letting her see it was him. She came over to the window and opened it. "What are you doing here?" she said. He waved his hand and pointed to the ditch behind him. She smiled and told him to wait over beyond the ditch and she'd be over. He could feel the excitement again. This time he had to fight with himself to keep it under control. He waited and waited and wondered would she ever come out. Then he heard a rustle behind him. She was creeping towards him, smiling. Her eyes shone. She was happy to see him. He couldn't wait any longer. He pulled her to himself and rubbed himself on her body, kissing and rubbing his hands all over, and even grabbing her breasts. She was pushing him and giggling at the same time. But when he unbuttoned his trousers and was tugging at her knickers she stopped. He stopped. She said to stop. But he couldn't stop anymore. He tossed her around and he was on top of her. But she wasn't laughing or giggling anymore. The excitement was about to explode but he wasn't finished. He was inside her when he exploded. She was kicking now, pushing him away, telling him to get off her, but he didn't care, he wanted to see her breasts. He pulled at her blouse. She wasn't wearing a bra. It was then he felt an awful pain in his groin. He let out a yelp and she pushed him away off her. "What…?" She kept saying, "What the fuck…" She was now on top of him punching him in the face. He tried to grab her but she managed to get to her feet and kick him once again in the balls. He doubled over with the pain. By the time he recovered, she was gone.

The following days and nights he didn't see her and he stayed away from the Kirwans. He went to the dance on the following Saturday night hoping he'd see her. Maybe she would ask him to come out again. But she wasn't there. He asked one of the lads whom he had met on the first night where she was. They told her she was probably in Athlone with her boyfriend. He lived there and she was probably 'out on the town' with him, they laughed and punched one another on the shoulder, "Sure ya know yerself."

He never saw her again. But every night, especially in Tullybeg when he was in bed getting ready to go to sleep, he thought about her and relived the excitement he got every time he thought of her from that first night, that night which he reckoned was the best night of his life.

Chapter 14

The summer was a busy one for Anne. Unfortunately, her mother took ill with a severe chest infection and she had to return home to help on the farm. Now that her mother was unable to do the housework and help out with the hay, it was an especially tense time in the house. Her father was a difficult man. Her older brother, Nicholas, and the father never got on. It was 'father's way or no way'. It came to the point where it got so bad Nicholas finally told him that he wasn't going to be bossed around anymore and that he had enough. He took the train to Cobh and ended up in New York. That left her two younger brothers at home trying to get on with their father, and a mother who could no longer keep the peace between them. Her mother was relieved when Anne walked in the front door.

"Thank God you're here, love. I don't have the strength to keep them from tearing at one another. The two lads will be the next to go if he's not careful, and then where will we be?"

Anne told the two lads to just do what they were told, get the hay saved, the turf in for the winter and then make whatever decision they wanted. But to, for Gods sakes, give Mam a break.

They agreed. But after one particular incident where a cock of hay tumbled from the cart and had to be forked back on, their father went ballistic shouting at the two lads. Anne was in the kitchen preparing the tea. The father shouted at them that they were useless gobshites and how did he have the bad luck to father such a shower of useless children. That was enough for Brian. He told his father to go fuck himself and that he'd be on the next boat to England. And, as Brian, told Anne, 'sure, wasn't it himself who forgot to tie down the fucking cock of hay'.

After the tea, Anne told the two boys to take a cycle into O'Callaghans for a pint. She knew that she needed to have a serious talk with her father and had been going over in her mind what she might say. But she never had a good relationship with her father. She was a girl. He had no respect for women. How her mother put up with him was always a mystery to Anne. But maybe she had no choice. She married into the farm. What alternatives did she have in her day? The boat to America, or England? The life of a spinster? He was considered a catch, or so her aunt Sadie claimed. Was she being sarcastic? How her mother's family thought Patrick Connaughton was a catch was a mystery. Often Anne thought maybe her mother was jilted or had a failed love affair and she was caught on the rebound. Or, alternatively maybe he was a better alternative than to what she had already. Her mother never talked about her past, and Anne was never really close with her mother's family, and except for the comment by Aunt Sadie, knew very little about her mother, only what she knew of her through her own experience. Given the present circumstance and the way in which her brothers rebelled against her father she was reluctant to think of her mother as weak or a bit of a mat. Maybe that was being unfair. And then gain, Anne had to admit that probably no woman, no matter how saintly or stupid, could put up with this man.

She rehearsed as many ways to begin the conversation or confrontation as she could. Imagined herself asking was it okay to have a word? Maybe make him a cup of tea and sidle her way into raising the issue of his sons and their attitude to him. She couldn't see those methods as being effective. He'd just brush her off.

When her brothers left the house, she found her father sitting by the fire reading the paper, and without any preamble, or asking him to listen to her, she launched into her father. She told him to cop on to himself. Hadn't he run Nicholas out of the house and now he's in New York.

"Now, girl, I'm your father and you don't be talkin' to your father like that," he said to her, his anger rising.

But she was ready for that. In fact, had anticipated it. She wasn't going to be intimidated. She wasn't going to be like her mother.

"I don't give a tuppenny damn about this place," she swept her hand around the kitchen, "but I do give a damn about Mam. And she has had enough of it. You either cop on to yourself or you will lose the two lads and then where will you and Mam be?"

He stared back at her, letting her know that she had no right to talk like that to him. But he didn't say anything.

"Well, what do you have to say for yourself, eh?" She wasn't about to let go, "You'd better say something or I, too, will leave this place and go back to Garrydangan. So bloody well make up your mind!"

She didn't wait for him to answer. She wasn't interested in his answer. He could take a run and jump for himself, as far as she was concerned.

Their father never apologised, but from that moment 'behaved himself', as their mother said. "Whatever you said to him worked."

By the end of the summer holidays, the atmosphere in the house had improved. They got the hay and turf saved, her mother had recovered and regained her old strength and managed to maintain control on their father's temper. But Anne didn't know how long it would last and would not be surprised if her mother wrote telling her that Brian and Aidan had up and left, and taken the boat.

All the while she was hoping to hear from Hubert. But there was nothing. They didn't have a phone so it would have been unfair to expect a phone call. And, as she reminded herself, he didn't have her Tipperary address. But it was still disappointing. They were getting on so well. She remembered their latest date (but it wasn't a 'date' as such); they went to see Synge's *Playboy of the Western World* at the Amateur Drama in Athlone. It was a really good production. Hubert was surprised at how professional it was. There were times he didn't understand the dialogue, he found it a bit odd. But when she told him it was Synge's translation of Irish into an English idiom he understood and admitted that there was some 'poetry' in it. This got them talking about poetry. She was surprised at his intelligence and his understanding of literature.

"For an army man, you mean." he teased.

"Well, I'm not surprised that you love Kipling."

He recited a good deal of *Danny Deaver*, or as he called it 'The hangin' of Danny Deaver'. But he could quote from Wilfred Owen and his favourite, Sassoon, as well.

He knew something of Yeats, and liked to quote the line, 'Romantic Ireland's dead and gone it's with O'Leary in the grave.'

"Certainly is," he said, "dead and gone."

She felt that there was a deep emotion, or sentiment, for him lurking beneath that particular phrase.

She introduced him to Kavanagh, and her favourite opening lines: 'Now leave the checkreins slack, the seed is flying far today…' It reminded her of her farming background. Kavanagh made it okay to love your local place, the farm you grew up in. The familiar could be turned to poetry. She loved that about him. There was a dark side to Kavanagh as well. And this she didn't mention to Hubert. While she was in Tipperary, she read and reread *The Great Hunger*. 'Clay is the word and clay is the flesh where the potato-gatherers like mechanised scarecrows…' The figure of Paddy Maguire was so real to her. She could see it in some of the bachelor farmers she knew. Kavanagh could have turned into one back in Monaghan, but he got out. Maguire reminded her of her father. Only for her mother, he'd have been another Paddy Maguire, only worse. At least, Paddy had some religious beliefs, had the farmer's spirituality, but her father had none. He went to Mass every Sunday, but probably wouldn't have even bothered to do that only for her mother. She felt sorry for him, but at the same time angry at what he had done to Nicholas and the two younger lads. How could there be forgiveness for that?

Hubert seemed to appreciate her taste, seemed to appreciate her. At least, she hoped so, and as the summer wound on through rain and worry and keeping the peace as best she could, Anne missed being with him and longed for telephone calls that could never be made and reading letters that would never arrive.

When she got back to Garrydangan, there was a letter waiting for her. It was from Hubert. Her hands were shaking with excitement, and a tear of joy had to be brushed away. It was a short letter, addressing her as 'Dear Anne', he apologised that he had not made any contact with her. She checked the date. It was a week ago. He informed her that he had been in England for much of the summer on 'legal and financial business'; that he would not have stayed much time in Garrydangan on any account, 'due to necessary consultation with his aunt, her solicitors and estate agents'. He promised her that when they met that he would explain in more detail matters he could not speak about but only in private.

She read and reread his letter, trying to plumb to his meanings and divining what he was telling her, and what were the things he wished to speak to her in private; there was joy and anxious anticipation in equal and unequal measure flooding through her all day.

On the following Monday of her arrival back into Garrydangan after the summer break, the school reopened. Louise O'Malley greeted her and welcomed her back. But she did not enquire as to her family, where or how she had spent the summer, only hoped that she had a good one and that she was rested and ready to meet the challenges of the school year. In turn, Anne was reluctant to ask how the principal's summer had gone and what she had been doing by way of relaxation. Both women merely nodded, in their familiar, chilled professional manner and each retired to their classroom.

Her children, however, were a delight. She greeted them and asked each of them how they spent their holidays and to tell everyone the best thing that happened to them. Most of the children had spent their holidays on their family farms helping with the hay, the hens, minding the dog, and for many the best thing was riding the horse, and being on top of the cart as the hay was being brought in. Others told of spending time with their Grannies 'down the country', which amused Anne, and one told how they had been to the sea-side in Tramore, but the weather wasn't great and the water was cold, but that the best thing was the bumpers and the wheel of fortune at the Fair.

Antoinette Keane put up her hand.

"Well, Antoinette, what is it you want to say?"

"I'm sad, Miss."

"Why?"

"Mammy told me that our neighbours, the Heneghans will be moving to England."

Anne's heart sank at the news, although she knew, it was still a blow to hear it confirmed.

"You'll miss them, of course, won't you?"

"Yes, Miss, and especially Doreen. My Mammy says she's lovely and she is too, Miss."

"I know, Antoinette. You're right, she is lovely, and we'll all miss her."

At the end of the school day Anne was sitting at her desk, thinking about Doreen and how sad she'd be to see her move to England. She heard a knock. She had to brush away her tears. It was Father O'Byrne.

"Good afternoon, Father." She recovered her demeanour and smiled at the priest.

He stood at the door, with that look she felt was meant for her alone. At least, he never seemed to be this way with Miss O'Malley or other people in the parish, or other women. Maybe he was just being a priest, and as far as her experience went priests had odd ideas about women, or at least behaved with women in very different way to ordinary men. But Father O'Byrne's manner with her, while always polite, was a little more than reticent. He wasn't reticent in the way Hubert was, whose reticence was based on Anglo-Irish background and of course his time in the army. Then again, Anne thought, priests joined a kind of army as well. But that wasn't what she felt either. When he came to the classroom to help prepare the children for First Holy Communion he was friendly, seemed to be happy with the way she was preparing them for the big day, but beyond those moments his look was almost intimate, or of one who desired an intimacy that he knew could not be pursued. Was that it? Was it some kind of repression of feeling towards women or even towards her in particular? It made her feel uncomfortable. He was older than her, maybe even ten years older, he was good looking, in a soft, timid sort of way. But she could see by his jowly face he would run to fat if he did not exercise and cut back on Mrs Daly's big dinners.

"May I have a word, Miss Connaughton?"

His voice sounded ominous, she was sure he was not going to deliver good news, or happy tidings. She indicated that this was, indeed, a good time to have a word, and she invited him to come closer. She stood so that he would not have to sit at a desk that would have been too small for him as she possessed the only adult sized chair in the room. So, they stood beside her desk.

"I wish to welcome you back to school, and hope you had a good holiday."

Anne said she had a good time with her family.

"Good, family is so important."

There was a silent moment which was at first awkward, but the discomfort of the silence was his doing. She would let him lead the conversation, after all, it was he who asked to speak to her.

"I want to thank you for all the work you put in last year especially with the children who were preparing for their First Confession and Communion."

Anne nodded, acknowledging the appreciation of her work.

"You have a remarkable way with the children. They seem to trust and admire you."

Anne again nodded her appreciation.

"They look up to you, seek from you a model of moral and Christian behaviour. It would be a great pity if this was undermined in any way."

Anne felt a knot of anger and anxiety tighten in her stomach.

He looked away, uncomfortable with what he was about to say, but letting it be known that it was his duty to speak. "I speak, of course, of your friendship with Captain Tyrrell."

A heavy silence hung all about the room. She heard a horse and cart clip-clop outside and a car (was it Hubert's?), in the distance. She told herself to be careful. To keep a neutral demeanour and put before the priest a blank face.

"Captain Tyrrell?" she managed to say with as much equanimity as she could muster.

"Yes. I'd like to remind you that he is a Protestant."

If this were her father, she would have let him have it. She knew what to say to him and she had the moral grounds on which to challenge him, but a priest was another matter; she didn't know what to say, and more importantly, how to say what she wanted to say.

"He, no doubt, is a good man, a man of principle, a Christian in his own way."

She was about to sniff aloud at the phrase, 'in his own way' but managed to control herself.

"And, no doubt I need not remind you that being a teacher in a Catholic school, one has certain obligations and responsibilities."

The silence had now been replaced with a low sounding buzzing in her ear. Was she losing her hearing? What else was he saying? She knew exactly what he was saying without hearing each word. Her job was on the line.

"I have a friendship with Captain Tyrrell." She heard herself say. "I do not see how this friendship should place an obstacle between me and my duties as a teacher."

"Quite. I am happy to hear that." He smiled and nodded to the floor, "But there are rumours. Rumours which, I am sure are only rumours, but nevertheless, as your curate and school manager, I have duties and responsibilities as well. To the parish, to the parents and of course to the children under your care."

A voice within her told her to say nothing more. Her body had tensed to the measure of a bowstring. It was best to politely get this priest out of the room as soon and as quickly as possible, lest she say or do something she would regret.

He bowed and left. She wasn't sure what his final words to her were. But no doubt even if he had said nothing more he had been plain speaking. No fraternising with the Protestants. No dating a Protestant. No relationship with a Protestant. No intimacies with a Protestant, under pain of expulsion or even excommunication.

Anne heard a noise outside the classroom. She was certain it was the principal. No doubt she had heard everything or, if not, at least knew why Father O'Byrne and herself were in conversation. She heard the school door clatter shut. The sound rattled off the corridor walls.

Chapter 15

Father Dan O'Byrne drove his black Morris Minor up the gravel avenue of the parish priest's house in Clochdroode. To his left was St Michael's parish church which stood on the promontory and, according to local historians, had given the town its name. Clochdroode, Druid's hill, or Druid's rock. Father O'Byrne was an avid reader of local history and was proud of Clochdroode's historical and of course, religious importance. It suited his view of the world that his parish church stood at the highest point and the most central position of religious significance in the county, and maybe even the diocese. The fact that the church was built on sacred ground that went back before the time of Patrick, probably even before the Druids themselves, added to the deep historical connection he felt with the Church, her institutions, her importance in the lives of, what he felt were, his people.

On getting out of the car, he saw that Father Leo Caffrey was in his garden. He was a tall, ascetic looking man, with thick grey hair, and he walked with a stoop. He wasn't vigorous but neither was he the sedentary type. His great love, besides the Church, was his garden. On seeing him again, Father O'Byrne recalled what his mother said of him when she heard that her son was being sent to work under Father

Caffrey. "He was trained in Rome, you know. Very bright. Bishop material, they say, anyone who is sent to the Roman College is marked for greatness." Her son took this as a sideways criticism of his 'failure' to be sent to Rome and yet not advance up the ladder of Ecclesiastical success. It was a blot in his copybook, according to his mother, and she reminded him every time she mentioned it. Which she now seldom did. But that didn't mean his mother had forgotten. The irony, of course, which was at least some comfort to him, was that his parish priest was never going to become a Bishop, he hadn't even been made a Monsignor. As far as Father O'Byrne could tell this hadn't bothered the old man in the least. It was well known in the diocese that Caffrey was bright but had more interest in a new species of rose than any recent document from the Vatican.

He greeted his parish priest and made his way to the garden where he was leaning over some roses.

"I see my floribunda are doing nicely," he greeted his curate with a nod, "they have great resistance, you know."

Father Dan didn't know what he meant.

"To disease. Very strong. Hardy. Just what you need in this climate."

Father O'Byrne politely agreed and said what a nice colour they were, and when a moment had passed and he felt he didn't have to admire roses any longer, he said, "Thank you for seeing me, Father."

"I got your note, Father." He moved towards another species, or was it the same? "Come sit down over here." He pointed to the garden seat which faced the town below.

"Well, Father, how can I be of help?"

"As you know we have had quite a difficult incident recently."

"Yes. Yes. You mean the migrants and all that. I heard what happened on Pattern Day. Disgraceful. I heard you gave a very good homily on the matter."

Father O'Byrne smiled with quiet pride. He hadn't known that word had reached the ears of his superior on the matter. "Thank you, that's very good of you to say."

"But we have to be careful, Father. We don't want to be getting into political matters and intruding on the secular divisions of our people. It's a difficult time of adjustment for us all, you know. I mean it's not just our parish that is having these difficulties. I'm with the government on this. My father was a Parnellite, and a Davitt man. The land must belong to the people. It's, after all, what we have fought for. And the west is too poor to bear its population. I'm sure you agree."

"Yes, Father. Of course. But the new influx of people is causing division and difficulties."

"I know, I know, Father, but they are good Catholics, are they not?"

"Yes, of course." Father O'Byrne was reminded of his parish visits. It was true that these households were among the most loyal to the teachings of the Church. The rosary, attendance at Masses and Benedictions, was heavily supported by these people. He smiled to himself with pleasure at the thought of Antoinette Keane's May Altar.

"I condemn violence at any time. And I was happy to hear that in your homily you spoke on the morality of the matter. You, as God's representative, must remind your parishioners of the law of God and, of course, in this case, the need to adhere to the law of the land. The Land Commission was set up to address an issue, namely poverty. We must always fight poverty, Father, for it undermines the stability of society and the Church. In time, with the new generations coming, all this will be forgotten. Families will inter-marry, have children, who in turn will become dutiful citizens and, of course, dutiful members of the Church."

"I agree, and hope that, as you say, in time, tensions and differences will ease. However, there is another matter."

Father O'Byrne told his parish priest of the rumours, the very strong rumours to do with one of his teachers, Miss Anne Connaughton, and her 'liaison' with a Protestant.

"And who is this gentleman?"

"Captain Hubert Tyrrell."

"It is indeed a serious matter, Father. We cannot have a teacher, one of our Catholic teachers, having relations with Protestants. It's bad for the children. It's a scandal to parents and to the people of the parish. How open is this relationship?"

"I must say that I myself have not seen them together. But I am reliably assured by someone who lives close to Miss Connaughton, that they have been seen together."

"In what manner have they been together? Are they living in sin?"

"I, er, I cannot say. But according to my sources they could very well be."

"So, it's not public, as yet?"

"No."

"And have you spoken to Miss Connaughton about the matter?"

"Yes." Father O'Byrne paused, carefully choosing his words, "I put the matter to her and informed her of her duties as a Catholic teacher, letting her know the implications of such a relationship."

"And has she quit it? Has she come to her senses?"

"Well, I can only say that my intervention was very recent, and I thought it a matter of justice to give her time to reflect on her position."

"It's most regrettable that this has happened, Father. We must give a clear and unequivocal message to our people, and more especially to the children in our care, that there is no salvation outside the one true Church. Protestantism is a heresy. It is an infestation that has eaten into the heart of our history. The English not only colonised our land, they colonised our souls with their heretical ideas. We, I mean, Rome, have been fighting it for centuries. We cannot allow our children to be infected with the presence of a teacher who compromises her faith. It is the very foundation of our society, Father. It is quite simply apostasy."

Father O'Byrne nodded in agreement. His superior articulated the very sentiments and beliefs he too held. It sent shivers down his spine to think that a child like Antoinette Keane who looked up to Miss Connaughton as a model Catholic would have to suffer doubts and confusions which would undermine her faith and place her soul in jeopardy.

The roses bent gently in the intermittent breezes and seemed to shine and bless both priests as they sat together.

Father Caffrey was silent for a moment and then asked, "Captain Tyrrell, you say?"

"Yes. He is the nephew of Lady Tyrrell."

"I am aware of the fact, Father. Which leads me to believe that maybe we are not in as much danger as we believe."

"Oh, how so, Father?"

"I know the Tyrrells, Father. And I have heard that she is in difficulties. She is deeply in debt. I need not tell you how I came about this piece of information. Suffice it to say that it is the duty of a parish priest to know what is going on in his parish. Not only religious matters but also non-religious. Needless to say, what I tell you is confidential."

"Of course, Father."

"I don't think we need worry too much about Miss Connaughton. I have it on good authority that Tyrrell House will have to be sold. That Captain Tyrrell would not have the means to buy it, and that it is more than likely that he will return to Dublin when the sale is finalised. Which means that, if indeed, Miss Connaughton and Captain Tyrrell do get married, she will have to give up her position as a teacher and, of course, leave Garrydangan. So, thank God, when she marries, she will be unable to teach anywhere, not even, it has to be said, in a Protestant school."

Father O'Byrne slapped his knee quietly and nodded. A solution had been found. No need to worry, and more importantly, no need to confront Anne Connaughton again. That was the biggest relief, as far as he personally was concerned. It would have been painful to have to face her and deliver the ultimatum. Thank God, as Father Caffrey said, for the law which restricted women from holding positions after they married. It made his life easier, and easier for all concerned.

But there was as yet another matter which Father O'Byrne wished to raise with his superior.

"There is a most delicate situation which I believe you ought to know about, father."

"And what is that?"

Father O'Byrne hesitated, he hadn't wanted to raise the matter but he had no choice. "It's about your niece, Miss O'Malley."

Father O'Byrne could feel a bristling beside him. Did he already know?

"What about her?"

Better to be direct, get it out in the open. "She is having an affair."

"Louise? Having an affair? Ridiculous."

"I thought it better that you heard it from me rather than from other sources."

"Are you telling me, Father, that there is a rumour, and nothing more, more substantial?"

"I'm afraid, Father I saw it with my own eyes."

"Saw what with your own eyes."

"Miss O'Malley has been most discreet. However, there have been occasions, more than one, or several occasions, when I saw her with Jamesie Roche."

"I know Jamesie. His wife died a few years ago. He has a daughter. I don't know how old she is. What do you mean she is carrying on an affair? They could be good friends. Nothing more."

"It is my belief that it is more than an affair."

"Your belief? So you have no evidence."

Father O'Byrne regretted raising the issue, but the situation had gone beyond what was acceptable, and if she and Jamesie Roche had been more discreet he might not, would not, have come to the conclusion that it was serious enough to warrant the parish priest, who happened to be an uncle, knowing about it. After all, as Father Caffrey had said, it was the duty of the parish priest to know what was going on in his parish. It was with deep regret that he had information about his niece.

"Josie Fagan," Father O'Byrne began.

"I know Josie, the post-mistress. A nosey gossiper if ever there was one."

"I don't doubt that, Father, but if she knows about it and is talking about it, then soon the whole of Garrydangan and eventually Clochdroode will know of it."

"Are you telling me you are relying on local gossip from a postmistress?"

"No, Father, if it was mere gossip, I wouldn't have mentioned it. But I've seen evidence myself."

"Evidence? You have evidence?"

"Well, more like indiscretions that I witnessed. By accident, you must understand."

"What did you witness, then, Father?"

"I saw them in Athlone together at a hotel. It was while I was visiting my family. They did not see me. I had come out of the Franciscan Church after first Mass. I was walking back to the house, where my mother was preparing breakfast. I saw them come out of the Regent Hotel together and get into his car."

Father Caffrey stood and walked a few paces, as if to clear his mind, "She can be a fool, at times. She takes after my sister, God be good to her. But why him, and why so public? Are they growing indiscreet, do you think?"

"All I can tell you is that Josie Fagan claims she saw them together in his car on enough occasions as to raise questions."

"Are they both fools? My God, why in the name of God doesn't she just marry the man? He's a widower. He has a child. What in the name of God are they thinking, carrying on like that in front of the child?"

Father O'Byrne did not tell him what Josie Fagan said to him about that particular issue. "That one is like all the Caffreys. She wants her cake and eat it too. Have a nice job, a principal's wages, a man to go to whenever she felt like it, a ready-made child, and her own house, to boot. Sure, she knows what would happen if she married him. Lose it all. She's not going to do that, she's too fond of her independence."

"This is the worst of all, Father. I appreciate you telling me. I will have to talk to her. She has to marry that man. That's all there is to it."

"But will she give up her job?"

"Father, I'm surprised at you. Surely, you of all people should not even be contemplating anything other than that my niece do the decent and honourable thing under the circumstances?"

It was getting chilly and Father O'Byrne was anxious to return to Garrydangan. He had come to speak with his superior under very difficult circumstances and needed to return to his house, to what was familiar and unchanging.

Father Caffrey walked him to the car, thanking him for informing him of what was going on.

"Do you not feel under siege, Father?" he asked his curate.

"What do you mean, Father?"

"All these troubles we as priests have to deal with on a daily basis."

The younger man said he did. "'The world is too much with us,' Father."

"Wordsworth, eh." He stopped turned to view the town and countryside below them. "Yes, too much with us. We have to stop it, Father. Our people will suffer, our children will suffer if we don't protect them. We are losing our Catholic values, I can see it. The wireless with its outside influences. And there's worse to come, you know. In America and in England, they have what they call television. I'm told it's full of paganism and advertisements promoting materialism. Rampant materialism, the Bishop tells us, and he's right, by God. I'm a man of the world, Father, don't get me wrong, but everything we talked about today, all the problems of the parish come from too much of outside influences contaminating our people. Films and music that isn't fit for Catholic eyes and ears. Remember, Father, we have to be constantly on the watch, reminding our people that there is no salvation outside the Church. It's a terrifying thought, but a true one. It's becoming easier and easier to slip unawares into hell. The devil is at work, Father. I see him and his works everywhere. We must be vigilant. Thanks be to God we have the Church to guard and protect us."

Chapter 16

On St Stephen's day Michael, the oldest of the Keanes, took a walk with his sister, Antoinette, along the boreen. They made their way to the Heneghan farm, as was their usual habit on the day after Christmas, only on this occasion the Heneghans had left for England a few weeks before. But they took a walk for old-times-sake. It had been a difficult time for Antoinette and himself. They both missed their visits to the Heneghans especially on St Stephen's Day, when Doreen and Mrs Heneghan would have sherry trifle and Christmas cake ready for them, and they'd be offered as much red lemonade as they wanted.

Michael missed them. Especially Doreen who although much older was very fond of him and he fantasised that if he had been older he might be 'calling on her' in the manner of a suitor. But it was a futile dream, but it pleased him nonetheless to have her nearby to look at and admire, not only for her beauty, but for her friendship. She always treated him as an adult and was never condescending, and of course Antoinette was always the favourite visitor.

Antoinette ran on ahead once they came to the sycamore tree which stood on the edge of the meadow field which in turn led to the garden of the Heneghan farmhouse. Instead of going in, as she normally would, she stopped at the gate. Michael thought this odd.

When Michael caught up with her he realised something was agitating her. Maybe it was the garden which was now overgrown and neglected, and the house was empty and as grey and still as winter. He remembered it as always well taken care of and smoke coming out of the chimney.

"Look," Antoinette was pointing at the windows. "They're all broken."

Michael's heart sank. The windows were indeed broken. Smashed with stones. Who would do such a thing? What vandal would come up here and do this?

Then Antoinette pointed at someone who was walking towards the hill field at the back. It was Frankie Dalton.

"Bloody, bastard." Michael shouted at him.

Frankie turned around and stood facing them, laughing. "Go fuck yerselves!" he shouted. "It doesn't belong to you."

Michael was about to run up to him and confront him. He knew Frankie wouldn't run, that he'd be delighted to have a fight. Michael was confident he could take him on. But he couldn't do that while he was with Antoinette.

"Bloody bastard, shouldn't be getting away with it," he said, "come on let's turn back."

Over the rest of the Christmas holidays Michael and his father would check the Heneghan farm. It was obvious that Frankie came here, probably at nighttime, and either stayed the night or found something else he could destroy. The front garden gate was pulled off its hinges; an old plough which the Heneghans could not sell was turned over and pushed into the ditch. The shed doors were closed over. They went in to check what damage was done. But there was little damage. In fact, it was rather neat and tidy. An old halter was hanging on a wooden hook as well as rope and old tins of creosote and half sack of barley. There was a chair that had the look of being sat in, and cigarette butts, as well as empty Guinness bottles strewn around the floor. Someone was here or came here on a regular basis.

They both looked at one another, they knew who it was.

By the end of the holidays, Frankie had returned to Tullybeg and no more damage was done. And yet they saw no one come to claim the farm and take it over. No one objected to the damage that was done. Why? Surely the new owners would have made objections and got the Guards involved. Did Garda John Holton know? Did no one go to him to complain?

It was Michael who voiced what his parents either did not want to, out of ignorance or out of anger. He knew his father was bitter that he didn't get an opportunity to put a bid on the farm.

"I think I know who bought the farm," he said one evening after supper. "The Daltons. They must have. It's why Frankie feels he can pull the place asunder. He knows his father didn't buy it to farm it."

"But why did he buy it, then?" Tomás asked.

"He has some plan. That bollix always has a plan."

Chapter 17

Mrs Grogan and her neighbour, Mrs Gilson, met Anne as they came out of Mass. It was the second Sunday after the New Year. Anne greeted them saying what a fine dry day it was for January and wasn't it a blessing that they had the frost instead of the rain. Anne smiled and agreed that she loved a frosty morning. Then they asked her if she heard anything about who bought the Heneghan land. She knew that they knew she was close to Doreen, and it would be a great coup for them to have some knowledge, from 'the horse's mouth', about the buyer. But Anne told them she knew no more than what anyone else knew.

"But you'd have other contacts," Mrs Gilson said, rather brazenly, which Mrs Grogan quickly added, "We don't mean any offence, Miss Connaughton, but we mean to say your landlord, it is rumoured, is involved."

Anne flushed, hoped it did not show, "I am quite sure I know nothing of the business. Good morning to you."

Anne walked back to her house and put on the kettle and heated the porridge. It was true about what she had told the two women, she knew nothing about who bought the farm, and Doreen never mentioned it in her letters. As to the reference to Captain Tyrrell, it made her uneasy that people, through local gossip, would find out about herself and Hubert. She took it on face value that what the two women meant was in fact true, that because she was paying rent to Captain Tyrrell, she might know something of what was the main topic of conversation.

On being reminded of Doreen, Anne's feeling of loneliness and isolation intensified. But there was nothing she could do about it and the only way to deal with it was by being stoical. It was a great emptiness in her heart to lose Doreen. In her most recent letter, she wrote that she and her parents had settled into Birmingham, that her uncle had been true to his word and already her father was happily working at something he enjoyed. Doreen herself had found work in a 'ladies fashion house' as she called it, and told Anne that she felt she had 'prospects', that her new boss seemed to like her and told her already that she had a 'lovely way with the customers'. Anne pictured the tall, elegant figure of Doreen with her bountiful red hair and open ready smile; she cried tears of joy for her success and tears of loss for herself. But in all the correspondences Doreen never mentioned who bought the farm. Perhaps she assumed that everyone knew by now, or she was under strict orders to say nothing. Anne assumed the former. Doreen was never one to be secretive and, as a matter of trust and confidence in their friendship, would have told her and requested she keep it to herself, for the time being.

But Hubert? Was it possible he knew and didn't tell her? But in this matter Anne was not sure and was unsure about her relationship with him.

She had finished the porridge and was standing at the kitchen window with a mug of tea in her hand looking out at the frosted garden. There was a still beauty about its whiteness, a purity to remind us of the possibility of heaven. It was so cosy to be inside, with a hot mug of tea and listening to the white winter silence. But inside her own landscape was far from silent. It buzzed with confusion and uncertainty.

She relived her meetings with Hubert. The times they met in Dublin, went to Bewley's Café on Grafton Street, her favourite street in all Dublin. Both agreed that a great deal of discretion was needed, especially after her interview with Father O'Byrne. Hubert was very understanding. In the past few months, he was rarely seen in Garrydangan, and only when there was business to be conducted. Rent money was simply posted into the Gate Lodge Office's letterbox, Anne kept a note of her payment and Hubert agreed to that arrangement. It was now their habit to meet in Dublin on Saturdays or Sundays whenever possible. She would take the bus from Clochdroode to Dublin, and on the Sundays, when they could meet, he drove down as far as Clochdroode and met her at the crossroads as was their old arrangement.

As she drank her tea and gazed out at the garden in her mind she was reaching for a summary of where her life was at the moment. Herself and Hubert seemed to get on so well together, there was an easiness and a warmth between them, but it never seemed to be at the level of intimacy she desired. What did she desire? Maybe it was she who didn't want a deeper intimacy. She couldn't quite fathom his feelings towards her. But she knew him to be the shy reticent gentleman type, she reassured herself. He wasn't going to push her beyond where she wanted to lead. He made this clear on the occasion when they discussed that fateful meeting with the priest.

Hubert understood the moral, or religious, as well as the professional, difficulties, Anne had to negotiate. He understood that as a Catholic, and especially a Catholic teacher, her position in society, or her local parish, made relationships with him, a Protestant, strained. He also knew the State regulation regarding married women holding jobs was also putting restrictions on her ability to be in a relationship with any man.

So, was he waiting for her to make up her mind about him, or was she uncertain of his love and feelings for her? 'Damn it', she said out loud to whatever spirits dwelt in the kitchen or whoever was the god, or goddess, of the garden. 'Bloody well make up your mind'. But whose mind needed to come to a decision was not certain. His or hers? And it was Sunday, the loneliest day of the week. How she missed Doreen and missed him as well.

On the following Monday, Anne happened to be in the post office where Josie Fagan, she could see, was only itching to talk. Two local women were in the queue, Anne was behind them.

"It'd be a sad day if an outsider got that farm." Josie addressed the two women but was looking at Anne.

To which the two women agreed. "'T would indeed."

"We've got to make sure that the land is given to one of our own. Isn't that right, Miss Connaughton?"

Why was Josie Fagan dragging her into the controversy? Did she not realise that as the local schoolteacher she had children from both sides of the local divide and was not going to get involved in these kinds of local disputes.

But Josie wasn't finished yet.

"We can only hope that the Heneghans did the right thing, and knew who needed the farm?"

"I'm sure the Heneghans sold to the highest bidder, Josie." Anne regretted opening her mouth.

"It's a lot more than about money, Miss Connaughton. Amn't I right?" she addressed the two women.

"We need to be getting over them kinds of divisions, Josie," Anne found herself saying. But she started so she would continue. It was her nature, "I'm sure a truppeny stamp is a truppeny stamp, Josie, no matter who buys it off you."

Anne regretted making the remark, but there was a deep satisfaction in the making of it, especially when Josie Fagan gave out an audible 'humpff' and handed out the stamps.

But she would have the last word. "All I'm sayin' is we don't want trouble around here. We've had enough of that in the past."

But Anne, as she walked out, couldn't let it go at that, "And let's keep it there, Josie, in the past."

Chapter 18

He smiled at how easy it was.

He had been checking her movements from different places for a long time now. Getting rid of the shed didn't stop him. It just made him more determined. Over the Christmas holidays he saw her at Mass and watched her, but he was careful never to be caught staring at her. He followed her she went back to her house after Mass and had her breakfast. He'd go behind the post-office and climb over the back-garden wall and then lay low on the low ditch behind her house. He'd watch her eating but he wouldn't stay long. He didn't want her to catch him. But he was laying out a plan. The more he thought about it the more the excitement grew, and sometimes his mickey would get real hard and he'd wait until he went back to his bedroom and think about her, and then he'd have the 'wet explosion'.

He would do it when he got out of Tullybeg for the Easter holidays. That would be the perfect time. He planned and rehearsed every detail in his mind.

On the Easter Sunday, he didn't go to Mass. He got into Anne's house by the back window. It was easy. The top window was always open. He had a stick ready to reach down and pull up the latch of the big window and he was inside.

He closed the window and went upstairs to her bedroom. It smelled of women's scent, and he opened her wardrobe and felt her clothes and they smelled nice. He could feel the excitement coming on him, but he knew how to control it so that he wouldn't have the explosion too early.

The front door opened, and he heard her light footsteps on the wooden floor. He heard her walking into the kitchen and moving about, filling the kettle from the tap. He could hardly contain himself. Then, at last, he heard light footsteps coming up the stairs. He stood behind the door. As soon as he saw her enter the room he couldn't stop himself, even if he had wanted to. He grabbed her from behind with one hand on her mouth to keep her quiet and the other around her body. She struggled with him trying to kick him, but he was too strong for her. He couldn't believe how light she was, and how strong his body was in comparison. This only intensified his excitement.

In one swift movement, which he had been practising in his mind, he managed to keep his left hand on her mouth, which she tried to bite but that didn't matter. The pain was part of the fun and he felt the excitement intensifying inside him. With his right hand, he pulled at her clothes. Her blouse ripped in his hands and he pulled at her knickers. He already had his trousers off, ready to throw her onto her bed. She kept twisting and turning her body trying to hit him, but it didn't matter. He felt nothing only his mickey full of the excitement and his body throbbing with desire and the effort to get his mickey inside her. He managed it. She kept bucking against him but it didn't matter. He felt the explosion go off inside her. It was over. He was satisfied. It was better than Phyllis.

The next moment that he was aware of was running down the back garden and making his way back to his bedroom without anyone seeing him. His mother shouted at him to get down to the shop and help his father. He checked himself in the mirror. He couldn't help smiling at himself with satisfaction. There was a slight bruise on his cheek, but nothing he couldn't lie about. His left hand was smeared with blood, but he could lie about that too.

Today was, without doubt, the best day in his life.

Chapter 19

Anne lay on the bed sobbing.

She could feel nothing. She was totally numb. Images of his face, laughing, snarling, his saliva dribbling onto her face, kept coming back, and coming back.

Then she felt sore down there and something in her mind told her to wash herself as quickly as possible. She didn't know if it would do any good. There was blood also, which only reminded her of the excruciating pain she felt. She kept washing and washing with soap and trying to get as much of him out as possible.

Then she cried and cried until she could cry no more. She cried out for her mother and then she thought of Doreen and cried out for her. But it was useless. There was no one there. She lay on the bed, her face covered with a pillow, and she screamed into it; she didn't want anyone to hear her.

That was the last thing she wanted.

One thing became clear in her mind, no one was going to know about this.

She knew she could not go over to the Daltons and tell them that their son had just raped her. He would obviously deny it, but even then, his mother would turn it on her, accusing her of seducing her son. She was the adult, he the child.

She knew how it would be twisted by the locals, even Josie Fagan, who ought to know her best. She was a brazen hussy, they'd say, who, out of frustration for not being able to marry a Protestant, was taking it out on young Dalton. She could hear them all, the whole village saying this.

She knew there was no point in going to the Guards. They would ask both of them questions. They would ask him what happened; at best he would lie and say that it was she who invited him into her bedroom; and she couldn't prove otherwise.

There would be no conclusive evidence of what happened, only her word against his, and his mother, and the village.

She also knew that if she told the Guards it would become public knowledge. And she knew that while some would take her side, most would go against her not because they had any pity for Frankie Dalton but because the story would be that she invited him into her bedroom. There was no getting around that.

She knew that Frankie Dalton would say nothing. He was stupid but he had an animal cunning. The most he might do was boast to his friends in Tullybeg what he did. They would believe him or not believe him. Mostly they would not believe him, claim that he was only boasting, trying to be the big man.

She knew that if she wanted to keep her job, or if she wanted to be with Hubert, she could never tell anyone, not the priest, not Louise O'Malley, not even Hubert, especially Hubert. If he found out, she would lose him forever.

She knew that her first instinct was the right one. She had to protect herself.

Anne lay in her bed until the tears subsided and she had found a space of calm; she had to take stock and plan her next move.

By evening she had taken a bath, put all the clothes she wore that morning into a paper bag and put it into the bin; she then got on her bicycle, made a phone call in Clochdroode, and by nighttime she was in Dublin with Hubert Tyrrell.

Chapter 20

Anne awoke in bed. Hubert was sleeping beside her. He was breathing steadily and was in a deep satisfied sleep. A sliver of light made its way through the heavy brown curtains. Outside, the Drumcondra street was quiet, the only sound was a distant lorry, possibly the milkman, although she didn't hear any clinking of glass. A burst of sudden wind rattled the window and she heard some paper, possibly an old newspaper, skate and tumble along the empty street. Anne couldn't find words to express the emotions swirling through her in the car on the way up to Dublin.

There was merely a set of facts, disembodied from time, place and feeling. Hubert didn't ask why she made the phone call, other to ask how she was. She said that she was feeling lonely, that she didn't like the idea of spending the rest of her school holidays in Garrydangan, and asked if that was okay.

He said it was. "Garrydangan is, after all, a major source of excitement and entertainment, too much for any sane person!"

She couldn't remember if she laughed at his witticism, or did they tease one another, or engage in banter. She only had facts, action and movement.

He boiled water to make a cup of tea and then asked if she would like some wine. They sat in his couch together and she moved closer to him. The rest happened quietly, gently and without rush, or overwhelming passion. They had sex, all the while he smiled into her face saying how much he had wanted this from her, and she said she knew. They kissed believing what they were doing was the most natural thing in the world for two people who loved one another.

Anne got out of bed and put on Hubert's bathrobe. He didn't move, he merely slept on, deeper than before. She went into the bathroom and looked into the mirror. She could not describe what she saw because she could not measure any emotional weight on scales that could register any of the events in her life over the past twenty-four hours. She became aware of the jewel-like quality of her green eyes. Was she beautiful? Her lips which had kissed his body felt somehow alive and soft. But there was something else she could not look at and she quickly turned away in disgust and returned to the bedroom but did not return to bed. She sat instead on the divan where some of their clothes were tossed, the rest were scattered on the floor.

Why had she done this? Was it really love, or was it something else? The silence of the room enveloped her and she sat not looking at what was in the room and only aware that Hubert continued to sleep quietly in the bed. Her ears became attuned to the outside, to the nuances of sound and particular noises she picked up like a wireless tuning into the ether beyond the room, the street, beyond the moment, beyond this morning.

She knew why she did it and it disgusted her. Her body hummed with the motor of guilt. It was guilt. If what happened yesterday had not happened, would she be here? If he hadn't attacked her, defiled her, raped her, would she have made the phone call? Would she be in the bedroom? Yes, it was wonderful to be here, but was it because of the sex, or the comfort Hubert gave her? Or, was this the inevitable event of lovers that would have happened anyway?

Anne quietly put on her clothes, making sure she didn't disturb Hubert, and made her way carefully and tensely down the stairs. She went into the kitchen and made herself a mug of tea with plenty of sugar.

Again, she sat in the silence thinking about what happened. She did it so that she could erase the body of her rapist from her being and replace it with Hubert's. That was the truth of it. She used Hubert to eradicate the disease that was Frankie Dalton. It was a sexual cleansing; it was a psychological cleaning, it was a moral cleansing, it was pure catharsis.

She shouldn't have done it. It spoiled everything. It knocked their relationship out of kilter. It knocked it out of whack despite the rightness of the act, despite the feeling she had of being with the right man. But it was the right man at completely the wrong time. There was a natural flow and movement in their relationship that was becoming an inevitability, but an inevitability that had its own pace and dynamism. The last twenty-four hours were like a dam, blocking what ought to be between them.

Hubert, naturally, would have expectations that she could not, at least as yet, meet. Or would he? He would see himself and Anne as a couple and would want it to be public and official. Or, would he? He would make demands of her that she could not meet. Or would he? As yet. Or ever? Then again, was not last night a sign that it was indeed time to declare her love, their love? He was so good and patient with her in the past; he had not forced anything on her that they might regret. He had been generous and showed nothing but tact and kindness to her. He came to Clochdroode at her bidding, did not demand any explanation, showed nothing other than consideration for her, wanted her to be safe and taken care of. Never asked why she phoned. He seemed to take it as a normal part of their relationship. How could she feel guilty? There was no need for guilt. What happened last night was inevitable, was it not? Would it not, even if it hadn't been preceded by that awful event? Surely, she should now accept the inevitability of it, the inevitability of their relationship moving in the direction it now had taken, he in bed upstairs and she down here in the kitchen drinking tea, in his house, what could be their house? The only difference being the timing of it?

Surely.

She should tell him what happened, she shouldn't lie, but she had made her mind up, she would tell him nothing. She would tell no one of what had happened. She would think and act as if it never happened. It never happened. It is erased.

There was a movement upstairs. He was getting up. She would wait for him to come down. They needed to talk, but she didn't know what to say or how to initiate the conversation. She hoped that when he came into the kitchen that it would become clear to her what to say.

Hubert walked into the kitchen.

"Tea?" she asked.

The erasement is now complete. We start again. We restart as of this moment.

"I know what we'll do today," he announced with a grin, as she poured him a mug of tea, "let's take the car to Dollymount, and we'll take a walk on the strand."

As they drove through Clontarf the sun rose light-gold behind thin squads of cloud. Hubert parked his car on the strand. It was empty and the tide was out. Howth Head gleamed a dough of brown bread in the morning sun. Hubert took Anne's arm and they walked not saying anything. He seemed happy to be out in the air, taking in the freshness of the morning with not a care in the world. She was happy to be with him; together walking

After about twenty minutes, Hubert turned to her, "Let's go back to the car."

On the return walk to the car, they didn't hold hands. Hubert led by striding as if he were in the army, moving with a purpose. Anne followed, happy with the opportunity to stretch the muscles of her legs and swing her arms and feeling a new energy in her body.

They got into the car. Hubert pulled out a packet of Players cigarettes and offered her one. She wasn't a smoker, but she took it. She had a sense that he needed a moment of distraction that he had something to say.

"You know that over the past year or so I've been busy with legal and financial issues."

"Yes, to do with your aunt."

"Yes. She has quite a deal of money to pay the tax man. To do with Tyrrell House and other properties she has in Dublin and London."

"Wow, I didn't think she had property in London."

"Yes, Kensington. A townhouse."

That sounded pretty grand to Anne. But there was more he wanted to say. She remained quiet, let him talk.

"I'm not sure how much you are aware of what's happening in Garrydangan."

"What do you mean?"

"I mean the Heneghan farm."

"No, nothing only that it was sold and that they decided to leave Ireland. Doreen told me."

"She didn't tell you who bought it."

"No. she didn't."

"Well, it was Dalton."

The name sent a shock of anger and fear through her body. The rumours were true.

"But it wasn't bought by him alone. I was involved. Me, Dalton and Holton. We are going into business together." He told her of the plan to open the quarry and set up a gravel and sand business for buildings, houses, and commercial properties.

"There is a problem, though. Tyrrell House will have to be closed. It's costing too much to run. It's a drain on my aunt's resources. It's also too near the quarry. Heneghan's land will be taken over and it will become the entrance and site of the new quarry business. Trucks and other equipment will be coming in and out of it. It will mean that I will have to move. Drumcondra will become my home. Rathmines where my aunt now lives will be hers until she dies. Then it will revert to me." He paused, looked at her, then turned away, "On condition."

Anne was following what he was saying. It seemed to her that he was telling her all this for a reason, and that it was to do with her. Was this going to be a proposal? A marriage proposal, or at least a plan for both of them until they knew what they wanted?

"There is a condition, Anne."

She looked at him nervously wanting to hear the rest but at the same time she wanted to tell him that she need not know. It was his business, nothing to do with her.

"My aunt has promised me the Dublin property. The Garrydangan houses that are rented out will have to be sold to help pay the tax bill."

So, that was it. He was about to tell her that she would have to vacate her house. Find other accommodation. She said nothing, waiting for him to finish what he wanted, or needed, to say.

"There's a catch, Anne." He looked at her.

"A catch?"

"I don't get the property unless I marry my cousin, Polly."

Anne wasn't sure she caught what he was saying. She heard marry, but the rest she quite didn't hear properly.

"Look, I'm sorry, Anne. It's a mess."

"Polly? Who is Polly?"

"She lives in London. Works there. Is a solicitor. She is also my aunt's brother's daughter. If all that makes sense. My aunt has, had, an only brother who had an only child, Polly. Aunt Constance feels obligated to take care of her, hence her codicil."

"Codicil?" Anne couldn't help laughing, "You mean she's a codicil?"

But Hubert wasn't laughing. He tossed the cigarette out the car window. "No, it's not like that at all."

Anne turned to look into his face, she tried to discern what she saw in his eyes. "So, where do I come in?"

"Look I'm sorry. After last night and all…"

"Forget last night. Who is this Polly, really? I mean, what is she to you? Is she merely your cousin or is she something more to you?"

He looked out the window of the car on his side, not wanting to look at her.

"How long have you known her? How long have you been together?"

"I tried to tell you, but…"

She looked out of the car window on her side. She could see Howth in the distance. It just stood there in the morning silence, brown, dun green, and behind, as a backdrop, a flat light blue sky. She tried to think of something to say, but her mind was blank. It was the wrong time to be blank, but maybe it was for the best. She would figure it all out later. But she wasn't angry at him, didn't feel like demanding explanations and desire to make a scene, nor was she sure she was being rejected for another woman. It really didn't register.

"I think you can take me home now. I mean I want to go back to Garrydangan if it's not too inconvenient. I'm sure there's a bus I can take."

"Look, I'm sorry. I should have said something."

"No. It's okay." And it would be okay.

He started the car and made his way out of the strand. They sat in silence all the way back to Drumcondra.

"I'll take you back to Garrydangan."

"No, Hubert, take me back to your house, I'll get my things and then you can take me to the Busaras. I'll be fine."

And it would be fine.

He sat in the car as she went into the house to collect her clothes and bag. He drove down Amiens Street and parked outside the bus station.

"Please, Anne, let's not break up like this. I need to explain."

"It's okay, Hubert, there is nothing to explain. It's just as well that I found out now rather than later, when…or, if we…" She got out of the car as quickly as she could, so there would not be a scene.

There was not going to be a scene.

She walked into the station without looking back. She went up to the kiosk and bought a ticket and as she took her seat, she saw that he was still sitting in the car where he had parked it. She did not turn to acknowledge him, or wave goodbye. She would never see him or talk to him again, never.

The CIE bus made its way out of Dublin and stopped in Chapelizod. There were about twenty passengers on the bus when they reached Enfield. Anne could not remember going through Maynooth and was surprised to realise she was less than an hour from Garrydangan. But her mind had not been on the scenery or watching the cows and horses in the green lush fields, or the people out and about in the towns and villages they passed through. It felt as if she existed in her own world. It was once again that disembodied world, without emotion, or sense of time or even colour.

"We lied to one another," she said to herself. "I lied to him, he lied to me."

She had wondered why she hadn't become angry at Hubert when he told her about Polly. She was angry, but, on reflection, not as angry as she could have been or even should have been. It revealed a lot, she thought. It also explained a lot. The lack of contact between them during the summer, he being busy with his legal and financial problems. He was in London for much of the time. This Polly lived in London. His 'reticence', as she had experienced it made sense, or at least she realised it wasn't just his 'army ways'.

He was a gentleman, she admitted that, he never pushed the relationship beyond where she wanted to go. This she had admitted to herself more than once. And then last night it was she who let him know that she wanted to sleep with him. Did she push herself on him, and was it that he didn't want to disappoint her?

But why hadn't she wanted to deepen the relationship, let him know clearly and honestly what she wanted from him? But she didn't. And when he told her about Polly she should have been angry, upset, should have screamed at him and told him that never in her life had she been treated so badly, so callously.

But, on the other hand, she didn't fight for him, didn't demand that he consider her as an obvious partner. She should have gotten out of the car and ran as far away as possible shouting at him that she never wanted to see him again. But she didn't. And the reason? What was the reason? Why didn't she?

She didn't know enough about Polly to make a judgement about her. What were his true feelings for her? Was it a matter of property, material gain, position and Class, overcoming his heart? Or maybe she, Polly, was the real deal, the true love of his life, and that his aunt's, the Lady Constance's, stipulation was merely a rubber stamping of what already was the case, the reality? If he put position and class over true love, then he didn't deserve her.

They had lied to one another, each for their own gain and each for the reasons most people lie, to protect themselves from pain, embarrassment, or the deep reluctance to face the truth, the ultimate truth about themselves, the fear of being alone, isolated, without companionship, the fear of facing the ultimate truth. I am alone. No matter how much we meet one another socially, no matter how intimate our feelings for one another, no matter the amount or intensity of our love making, there is a knowledge in the heart, or the soul, that we are ultimately alone. The heart's ultimate and core knowing and wisdom. Even last night's sex, though wonderful and exciting and full of promise as it had been, was based on a lie. Her lie. Having sex with Hubert, a good and as honourable a man as he could be, given his circumstances, could not blot out the stain of that other evil. That malignant presence in the village; he, the personification of the evil that lies at the heart of Garrydangan.

Anne felt nauseous on the bus, it wasn't travel sickness, it was the thought of him, the utter mindless violence she experienced at his hands; the anger she felt at herself for not being able to stop him. The anger she felt at how he was able to do what he wanted and there was nothing she could do. She wanted him dead. She not only wanted him cleansed from her body, eradicated from her feelings and from her soul, she wanted him dead, physically and finally, dead. If he was sitting in this very bus now, sitting in the back seat with those men now, she would, this very second, take out her nail file, her pencil, her small scissors, and would, without any feeling of bad conscience, without a second's hesitation, without any feeling of regret, even knowing that she could be arrested and put in gaol, she would get out of her seat and attack him, gouge his eyes out and then stick the scissors between his legs and rip his member. She would make sure she hit an artery so there was no hope of him recovering. She would feel total elation at seeing his blood flow out from him and soak his trousers and drip, drip slowly and relentlessly onto the floor of the bus. Yes, she told herself, she would. There was not a moment's doubt in her mind that that is exactly what she would do.

It was late afternoon when the bus dropped her off at Clochdroode. She picked up her bike which lay against the wall at the back of McElroys and cycled back to her rented house in Garrydangan.

Chapter 21

The Easter holidays were over. Anne was back at school. She did her best to be as normal as she could in the classroom. Her children deserved that she maintain her professional standards. She managed to muster up as much fun and brightness as before. The children were delighted to see her back. She asked them what they did over the Easter; she laughed with them; scolded when necessary.

But when she got back to the house, she was exhausted. The classroom drained her.

On Wednesday, she was on lunch duty in the yard. As usual the children were playing in groups. She noticed that in one group Moya Roche was surrounded by a number of girls who seemed to be worried about her. As discreetly as she could she went over to them and asked if everything was alright. Bronagh Delamere, Moya's best friend, said that Moya had been crying.

"What's the matter, Moya?" Anne asked gently.

Moya looked away. She didn't want to tell her.

Anne asked the girls to return to their classrooms, that everything was fine; that she would speak to Moya.

Anne took Moya's hand and brought her over to the wall at the side of the school where no one from any of the classrooms could see them.

Moya Roche was ten years of age and was in Miss O'Malley's class.

"Is there something you want to tell me, Moya?"

Moya shook her head. No there wasn't.

"Then why are you crying?"

Moya could not hold it in any longer she put her thin arms around Anne and cried as if looking for protection.

"What is it?"

Moya couldn't say.

"Would it be better if you talked to Miss O'Malley? She's the principal; she might be able to help you."

At this, Moya cried all the more, shaking her head.

Miss O'Malley was now standing at the top of the yard, "Moya Roche," she called, "come into your classroom, at once."

Moya did not hesitate; a look of horrifying fear came over the girl's face. She loosened herself from Anne and ran back to the classroom.

Anne walked behind her. Miss O'Malley remained standing waiting to speak to Anne.

"Miss Connaughton, I'm sure you have a class to attend."

Anne was stunned into silence. She wanted to yell at her that Moya was obviously upset, and all she was doing was trying to help the child. But at the same time, she knew she was wasting her time. Louise O'Malley was not going to listen.

At the end of the school day when all her children had been dismissed, Bronagh Delamere and Moya Roche knocked on Anne's door. Bronagh was holding Moya's hand.

"Miss, Moya wants to talk to you."

But Moya shook her head and told Bronagh that she didn't.

"Yes, you do," Bronagh pulled Moya into the room.

"Come, sit down here, girls," Anne invited them to sit at her desk.

Bronagh made sure Moya was sitting and then said, "I have to go, Miss. My mother is waiting."

Anne sensed that Moya was ready to talk. She assured Moya that she could tell her anything, and that it was alright.

Moya told her.

Anne wasn't sure she heard Moya correctly. She thought it was going to be about someone bullying her, or about feeling sorry for herself because her mother died when she was younger, and maybe she was missing her. But she wasn't expecting to hear this.

"Tell me gain, Moya."

Anne, this time, was going to make sure she heard every word.

Moya was reluctant. She didn't want to have to say the things she had already said.

"It's okay, Moya. I just want to hear it from you again."

"My dad makes me sleep with him and he does things and I don't like it."

"What things?" Anne didn't want to know, but she knew she had to know, otherwise she wouldn't be able to help her.

"He puts his thing inside me and it hurts."

Anne's mind went blank. She stared at Moya, trying to control the shock. She was horrified. Moya needed her to be calm. But all she could see was Moya's face in pain and crying, crying all night. Nausea almost overwhelmed her. She was back in her own bedroom when she was attacked. She grabbed the edge of the desk and squeezed as hard as she could, so she felt enough pain to stay in the moment and be with Moya. Without realising it she was holding Moya in her arms and both were crying. She didn't want to let go of this poor child. She wanted to hold her and protect her for as long as was needed. But she had to let go.

She had to figure out what to do. She had never been in a situation like this. She had never been told about anything like this ever happening before. Her head was spinning, trying to cope and to decide what she was to do next. How could such a thing happen between a father and a daughter? She stood up from the desk and suddenly became very dizzy. She sat back down. How could a father do this to his own child?

She had to tell the principal. She had to know. Anne had to tell her. This was not something you could keep to yourself.

She asked Moya would she be okay by herself for a few minutes that she would come back shortly.

Louise O'Malley was in her classroom putting some papers into her bag, ready to leave.

"What is it, Miss Connaughton?"

"I have Moya Roche in my room. She's very upset."

"About what?"

Anne hesitated, she didn't know what to say or how to say what she heard.

"Well, Miss Connaughton, I don't have all day."

"Moya says that her father forces her to sleep with him." Anne couldn't say the rest. She couldn't find the words.

"Nonsense."

"I'm sure she's telling the truth."

"How do you know? She's a liar. I know the girl. She's in my class. You don't know her. She tells stories about other children. Gets them into trouble. She's a troublemaker."

"But, I don't think she's making this up."

"What do you know about her?"

"She's crying and very upset."

"She's just looking for attention. Where is she? I'll speak to her."

Anne regretted she had said anything to the principal and reluctantly led her back to her classroom. Moya was still sitting at the desk, crying.

When she saw Miss O'Malley, she visibly whitened. She looked at Anne as if she had betrayed her. Anne felt her betrayal in the pit of her stomach and knew she had made a catastrophic mistake. But what else was she to do?

"What kind of lies have you been spreading?" Miss O'Malley shouted at her, "Get out of here and go home, and let me not hear more lies from you."

Anne felt another blow to her solar plexus. What did she do wrong? This should not be happening.

"Now, Miss Connaughton, my advice to you is that you disregard what you heard from Moya Roche. She is a known liar and whatever she tells you, cannot be taken seriously." She turned and left the classroom.

The next day, Bronagh Delamere came to Anne during lunch break and told her that Moya wasn't in school. Anne asked her did she know why. Bronagh said she didn't know.

Only that her father kept her at home because she wasn't feeling well.

Anne noticed that Moya wasn't in for the rest of the week, and when she came to school on the following Monday Anne walked towards her in the yard during lunch hoping she would let her have a word. But Moya put her head down and walked away. For the next few days, Anne noticed that Moya kept to herself. She managed to get a moment with Bronagh and asked her about Moya. Bronagh told her that Moya didn't talk to the girls anymore.

Chapter 22

Mrs Daly came into the dining room while Father O'Byrne was having his tea.

"Miss Connaughton is here to see you, Father."

When he went into the parlour he was shocked at what he saw. Miss Connaughton looked thin and very tired. Her eyes had darkened, that green lustre had dimmed; some great pain resided within them.

"Are you okay, Miss Connaughton? Will I get some tea for you?"

"No, no, Father, I'm fine."

But he had already left the room and gone into the kitchen. "Will you bring a pot of tea for us, please, Mrs Daly."

When he came back, Anne was sitting at the mahogany table, a little stooped, staring at her hands, rubbing them together.

The priest felt sorry for her. Her normally healthy face looked ashen and dry. He had an impulse to sit beside her and take her in his arms, but he couldn't do that. He brushed away the thought, his mind tingling with guilt; he couldn't allow himself to weaken in this occasion of sin.

"Miss Connaughton, what can I do for you?" He said stiffly, now in control.

She was about to speak when Mrs Daly came in with a tray of tea and biscuits.

Mrs Daly realised from the first moment she saw Miss Connaughton at the door that something truly serious must have happened. It was annoying that she couldn't take a seat with them and listen. She reluctantly nodded to Father O'Byrne, who thanked her for the tea, and told her he would look after things now.

He poured tea and placed the milk, sugar and biscuits beside Anne, but she didn't even look at them.

Father O'Byrne sat opposite, placed his hands on the table and joined them as if in prayer. "What did you want to see me about, Miss Connaughton?"

It took a few moments but eventually she lifted her head towards him and told him that she was worried about a pupil in the school.

"I see. Tell me more."

The only reason why Anne had decided to see the priest was because there was no one else she could speak to, and she needed to talk to someone and because he was the ultimate authority in the school, he was the manager. He was the one ultimately responsible for the welfare and wellbeing of the school.

She told him exactly what Moya had told her. She had it almost verbatim. It was as if she had written it all down to learn it off by heart so she wouldn't have to feel it.

As Anne related what Moya told her the priest's body became numb. Both his hands were now fists, he didn't realise this until he felt the pain in his knuckles. His heart squeezed in pain and his breathing had almost stopped. He had never heard anything like this in his life. He didn't know what to say, he didn't know what he was feeling; only his body told him that something terrible had happened to this child, but his mind could not comprehend what the body was saying. The first thought, or picture, that came to his mind was his mother. If he told his mother what he had just heard, she would not believe him. Things like this just did not happen. So, was what he was hearing true? Could something like this really happen?

The room darkened. But was that because it was late evening or was it his imagination? Was the darkness of all the events that had been taking place since Pattern Day now finally overwhelming him. As a priest he had never expected to be overcome by the evil within the world.

"I'm sorry, Miss Connaughton. Could you please, tell me again what you heard from this child?"

She repeated verbatim without emotion, but he knew that it was a dampened down emotion. He realised that she was feeling as disturbed and confused as he. She, too, was drained of feeling.

They sat in silence, the room had attuned itself to their frightened and confused presence.

Father O'Byrne needed to find a word, it was vital to him to find the right word so that he would have something to grasp, to hold him and give him ballast; he searched his mind, but he couldn't reach the word he was seeking. He looked into Anne's beautiful but now pain-filled face to see if she would help him. But he turned away, fearful that he would say something, or even do something, which he as a priest was never allowed to do or say. His mind became a whirl of frenzy. It was better to be in a chaotic frenzy than actually thinking about what he had been told.

"Are you sure, Miss Connaughton?" he asked, not looking at her. He could not afford to look at her. He needed to be strong. "Could it be possible that this child is lying, or making it up?"

"How could a child make this up, Father?" Anne raised her head and looked at him, the deep emerald eyes dark and full of anguish, "how could a child be able to describe what I've told you unless it actually happened?"

She looked into his eyes without flinching, pleading with this priest to take her seriously.

He turned away; he couldn't bear to see this woman in such pain. His feelings for her could not be admitted. He could hear himself telling himself that there was grave danger in this admission. He was aware of himself reminding himself what he was, a priest. Though he still had doubts about what had happened to this child, he was convinced because Anne was convinced and, as her priest, and in the capacities he knew her, he knew she was not someone to fabricate, or lie, or to twist and form an event into something to suit her own opinion or point of view. He knew she was no creator of melodrama or gossip.

"Yes, Miss Connaughton, you are right. How could she."

He thought of his father, who was a solicitor, who dealt with people all his life. Had he ever come across something like this? What about the parish priest? Even if they hadn't, and he could not be sure, for he was too young and inexperienced to know, he asked himself, what they, his father as a solicitor, and Leo Caffrey, as an old experienced priest, would do at this moment? What advice would they give him?

"What do we do, Father? What do we do?" Anne was holding back a dam of tears that were straining to break loose.

It was then that he connected Moya Roche with Jamesie Roche and what he knew about the relationship between him and Louise O'Malley. He was so overcome he held his head in his hands. Did Anne Connaughton know? Could he tell her? He struggled to hold back the tears. He couldn't show Anne any weakness. He was a man of God, he had to be strong.

And did Louise O'Malley know what was going on? How much did she know? What would happen if she knew what he was doing?

"You have done the right thing, Miss Connaughton, in coming to me."

"I told the principal, as was my duty, Father. She has done nothing about it. In fact, she says the child is lying, has made up the whole story. I come to you now as the Manager. You have to do something about it."

"Look, all I can do is report what you told me to Father Caffrey. He is the ultimate authority in the parish."

"But the Guards, John Holton has to be told."

The room darkened even more. Maybe he should put on the light, but he couldn't move. He didn't want the light on, he needed to be enveloped in darkness. He needed to think this through with her. His thoughts were coming together, his brain was quietly allowing his mind to form some kind of clarity.

"Would that do any good?" He asked.

Anne was shocked. "What do you mean? Of course it would."

"Think about it for a moment, Miss Connaughton. What would she say? Would she want to, or agree to, tell the Guards?"

"I'll back her up. I'll tell them."

His mind was clearer now. He was thinking as if he were his father, the solicitor.

"That won't be good enough."

"What? What do you mean? Of course they'll believe me."

"But your word doesn't matter, Miss Connaughton. The child will have to make a statement. The question is, will she? Even if what you say is true, what will her father say? He will be asked to make a statement as well. He'll deny it. Call his daughter a liar. Who will the Guards believe? Who will believe the word of a child over an adult?"

It was exactly Louise O'Malley's response.

"Oh, my God. The poor, poor child."

She told Father O'Byrne about how Moya wouldn't even look at her in school. "Her father has too much power over her." Anne's head slumped helplessly, "She'd never say anything against him."

Suddenly she burst into uncontrollable tears. Her body shaking with pain, her mind distraught.

He pushed down his instinct to go over to her and sit beside her and hold her. He held his body back, his arms stretched out on the table, his fingers digging into the wood. He wanted to reach out and console, but he needed consolation too, and this woman would give it to him, if only he asked. She was that kind of person, kind and loving, had such a good heart. Loved her children so deeply, she might even love him. He was in need of her love as much as they. But he looked away. The veil came down. The door was shut. It could never be, and he could never allow it.

He stood and walked to the window and gazed out at the night. The beech tree was swaying. He could hear the wind blowing through it. Was it a keening sound, a dirge for us all; for me, for Anne, for poor Moya?

"She's trapped, Father. Trapped."

He pictured a rabbit's leg, iron clamps biting into raw bone and the excruciating pain the helpless animal was going through.

"The poor, girl." She said, "The poor girl."

Father O'Byrne turned around and looked at her. She was so vulnerable, and so beautiful. His heart ached for her, but not only for her but for himself. He was not allowed to seek consolation from this young woman; he ached for the ten-year-old innocent child who had to live with a monster. Trapped, yes, trapped was the right word. Forever.

And what could they do now? They were powerless. They too were trapped. No one was going to believe her, or them, he knew.

He was priest long enough in Garrydangan to know that if he accused Jamesie Roche of these appalling acts he would be criticised for believing a child over a father. That was a stark truth. They, the people of the parish, would claim that he had something against the Roches. The Roches were here longer than he was. The Roche's went back generations, he was a mere blow-in, a passing bird, someone who could be replaced. Even if they believed him, or even if some believed him, it would divide the parish.

And what effect would it have on the child? What future would she have in the parish if everyone she met, and talked to, knew what had happened. They would avoid her, ostracise her; say awful, cruel things to her and about her. Her life in Garrydangan would be a purgatory.

No one in Garrydangan was going to do anything about this. And even if they did know, what could they do about it? To know something was one thing, but to know the truth didn't matter. Knowing the truth didn't achieve anything. It just left them powerless, totally helpless.

He knew, and he suspected that Anne knew also, that nothing would be done about this. Each person, each family in Garrydangan would just pull back, like snails into its shell and go on with their lives, because they knew that they too were powerless. It was a private matter, it was a family matter, and you did not interfere with families. Didn't every family have its secrets. Was that not the one thing he learnt about Garrydangan from the secrecy of the confessional box. Alcoholism. Violence against mother and children. Hatred of bosses and fellow workers, the very bosses and fellow workers they went to Mass with and received Communion with. Family secrets told inside the sacrament, and then denied outside. Everyone pretending their family was a model of Christian virtue. And the gossipers and the scandal tellers, the very ones whose secrets cannot be revealed, so a veil of pretence, the empty sepulchres abided, always abided. Our Lord was right about the Pharisees and the tax-collectors, but we'd be wrong to believe they no longer exist. Hypocrisy and denial, that's how a village like Garrydangan is sustained.

Father O'Byrne sat down again in front of Anne. She had composed herself and it was now she who was looking out into the night.

The only words that came to him were the Our Father and the Hail Mary. He prayed the words silently. There was nothing else to say or do.

He sat with Anne until she was ready to leave. He would sit with her, gladly. This was the consolation he needed. He was her priest, it was his duty to be with her, as with each of God's sons and daughters, to be with them in their suffering; but couldn't admit that he needed her to sit with him, too, to be with him in his. Their mutual silence was an inadmissible bond.

Chapter 23

Antoinette was too sick to go to school. She complained of a pain in her stomach. At first, her parents were not concerned but on the third morning became worried and asked Dr Travers to make a call. He examined her. Her temperature was not unduly high, the pain in her stomach did not indicate an appendix, nor did her internal organs indicate any kidney, liver or stomach problems.

He asked her parents did anything happen recently which might have upset her more than what was usual.

At first, they couldn't think of anything. Then Sylvia said that Antoinette became very upset when Miss Connaughton, her teacher, left the school.

"Oh, when was this?" Dr Travers hadn't heard anything of the matter.

"Yes, it was very sudden, Doctor." Sylvia explained as she poured him a cup of tea and offered him some biscuits. "She's gone to England."

"Why?"

"We don't really know, Doctor. But Josie Fagan, says it was something to do with Hubert Tyrrell."

Doctor Travers knew of the Captain, had heard that he was involved in some local business venture with Frank Dalton.

"I see."

"She's a gossip, that one, spreading rumours."

"Rumours?"

But he stopped her before she said anything more; he guessed what the rumours could be.

"Poor, woman," Sylvia was rubbing her wet hands on her apron, "sure, we all loved her; and when we heard about her leaving, poor Antoinette was heartbroken."

Tomás, who had just come in, was standing at the door, ready to go out and continue to milk the cows, said, "Heard that Miss Connaughton and himself were great together."

Sylvia looked at him in admonishment, "We don't know that, Tomás, we can't be going about spreading rumours."

Tomás made a face that said, 'things happen'. "Anyway, Antoinette loved Miss Connaughton, and she doesn't like the new one."

"She's grand, Doctor. You probably know here. She's Donie Riordan's daughter from outside Clochdroode. She came highly recommend to Father O'Byrne." Sylvia said, "Antoinette just needs to get over it. She has to go to school, and that's the end of it."

Doctor Travers stood to go, "You're probably right, Mrs Keane. She'll get over it, children are resilient. Give her another day and send her in. I'll prescribe a tonic, in any case, she needs her iron and vitamins."

The following day Sylvia sent Antoinette into school. And for the next few days she was sent to school. When she came back in the afternoon, she told her mother that everything was okay, and that Miss Riordan was nice.

On Tuesday of the following week, Michael Keane was down the river field after the cows were milked. There he discovered Antoinette by the stream, sitting in the hedge which was shaped like a cave and that she used to play 'house' with her dolls.

"What are you doing here? You should be at school." He went over to her.

She was sitting with her back to him, arms wrapped around her knees. "I can't. I don't want to."

"Were you at school today?"

She shook her head.

"What about yesterday? Last week?"

She didn't answer.

"God, Antoinette, what's wrong?"

"I want to talk to Miss Connaughton, but she's not here anymore."

"What do you want to talk to her about?"

She looked at him appealing to him to help her. But he didn't know how.

"I want to talk to her."

"But, she's in England, Antoinette." He was annoyed that he couldn't help her, but he had an idea. "Would you talk to Father O'Byrne?"

"Would he know where she is?"

"I'm sure he would," Michael was desperate to say anything that would help his sister, and get her to talk to someone, anyone. "He might even be able to contact her for you."

Father O'Byrne drove up to the farm. Tomás and Michael, were waiting. They greeted him, thanked him for coming, talked about the car, and what a great engine the Morris Minors had, so well built it would run for years.

"She's in the house, Father," Tomás nodded towards the house, "but I'm not sure you can help her."

"Oh."

"She wants you to find a way to get Miss Connaughton to talk to her."

"About what?"

"We don't know, Father," Michael, said, "I've been asking her and asking her and she won't tell us."

Sylvia Keane welcomed him with a grateful smile, "Thanks for coming, Father. She's in her room."

Antoinette was sitting on her bed fully dressed. She didn't look at Father O'Byrne as he sat on the chair beside her. She was stroking her doll, as if soothing it. Father O'Byrne looked around. His heart sank when he saw the Altar. There were no flowers and the head of Our Lady was broken and glued together with Bostick, its brown uneven ring a shabby necklace.

"What happened to Our Lady?" He asked gently.

"It fell."

"And who fixed it?"

"Michael did it for me."

"Do you still pray to her?"

She shook her head. Then, not to disappoint, "Now and again."

A sadness came over him. He felt a loss. Antoinette had been his favourite communicant. He had such hope in her, he delighted in her innocence, her open smile and realised he missed the cheerfulness she radiated whenever he saw her.

"Michael tells me you wanted to talk to Miss Connaughton."

"Where is she?"

Father O'Byrne did not want to think about Miss Connaughton. She had let him down, had let her children down. She had just run off. She came to him in the parish house and told him that she was leaving and would be going to England. He had asked why. She looked at him. 'Are you going to him?' he had asked. She merely looked at him, apologised for the inconvenience, thanked him, and left. He was angry at himself for not being able to get her to talk, to open up. He loved her, wanted to help her, but he was a priest. It could not be. He brushed aside the image of her; she would be of no help now.

He couldn't say anything of this to this child. It was something she might understand later, much later.

"She's in Birmingham," he said simply. He had found out through Tim Dooley who had always been friendly with the Keanes.

"Why? Why did she go to Birmingham? Did she not like us anymore."

"No, Antoinette, it wasn't that."

"Why didn't she say goodbye and tell us she was leaving?"

"She couldn't. She had to leave early. She was very sorry not to have had the chance to say goodbye."

Antoinette was crying now, hugging her doll to her chest. "I need to talk to her."

His heart broke watching her. There was nothing he could do; with all his priestly powers, his prayers and the sacraments, what was he to do to help this child?

"Maybe if you told me, I might be able to help," he finally said out of deep desperation.

She turned for the first time to look at him. It looked like Miss Connaughton could not help her, she was too far away; and she remembered the priest coming into the class when Miss Connaughton was there and how she seemed to like him, and how they had knelt in front of her May Altar and prayed together.

Finally, after hesitation, she nodded.

She told him.

Father O'Byrne had to gather his thoughts before he left Antoinette's bedroom and went into the kitchen.

Sylvia, Tomás and Michael were waiting, hoping that the priest would tell them that Antoinette was fine and everything was okay.

"Well, Father?" Sylvia asked, her tired, strained face pleading and hoping.

"I think you should go in to see her," the priest said to her. He indicated to the two men that he wanted to speak to them outside. "Let her have time with her mother," he said to the two men.

The priest walked back towards his car, the two men followed not a little anxious.

"For God sakes, Father, tell us, what did she tell you?"

The priest stood at his car. He was still in shock.

"For God's sakes, Father what is it?" The two men pleaded in desperation.

Finally, he could speak, but all he could say was, "Frankie Dalton."

At the mention of his name, Tomás grabbed the priest roughly by the shoulder, "What did he do, Father?"

The priest fought back tears; his voice strained.

"He…. She told me…." He could hardly say the word, "He attacked her…"

"What do you mean, 'attacked' her?"

Father O'Byrne couldn't form the words, but they looked at him and somehow divined what he was trying to tell them.

Tomás and Michael turned and ran into the house. Sylvia was standing in the kitchen, trying not to break down, trying to be strong for her daughter and her men. "Yes, she told me."

But it was too much. She collapsed into the arms of her husband and son.

Chapter 24

On the following day, Father O'Byrne visited the Keane family. The two men sat in the priest's car outside the Keane house.

"How is she?" the priest asked.

"She still won't go to school, but at least she's not hiding in a field somewhere. She's not the same child, Father. She cries and won't leave the house. It's not safe for her."

From where he was sitting, the priest could see the top of Heneghan's shed where he attacked her. All she was doing was checking on the house to see who had moved in, not realising that it would never again be occupied. He knew that. He knew who owned the property. Told her she was trespassing, but he wouldn't tell the Guards if she did what he told her.

Father O'Byrne's anger was such that he could hardly admit to himself the depths of it. Priests are not allowed to feel such uncontrollable chaos in themselves. They were expected to have the mind of God, and the mind of God took the eternal view, sought equanimity; had eyes only for what lay beyond this world. But he was a man, he was human, and his anger was rooted in a fact that he could not pull beyond this world and place it at the eternal feet of God. His human anger was rooted in the knowledge that Frankie Dalton was going to get away with it. Just as Jamesie Roche would be getting away with what he did to his own daughter, and for the same reasons that Anne and himself had talked about less than a month ago. And he knew Antoinette's father, who was sitting beside him, knew it. Dalton would get away with it.

There was no way, Tomás had told him that they, he and his wife and the two lads, would tell anyone. There was no way they were going to allow Antoinette to have to face the people of Garrydangan and have the whole village talking about her and about them. Tomás and Sylvia knew what the people in the village would say: How they were bad parents for not protecting their child, that they didn't keep an eye on her; that it was their fault that he was able to talk to her; they should have made sure he never got near her; and he and Sylvia knew that somehow 'they' would find a way to blame their daughter for letting it happen. They would say that she should have 'run away from him', 'never have gone near him', 'just run away and it wouldn't have happened'. That's what they'd say. With no conception that that was asking the impossible from a seven-year-old child.

Father O'Byrne suggested that the Daltons should know what their son did. "They need to be told what kind of person he is," he said. "They need to know."

"Do you think they would listen, Father?" Tomás had answered, "Do you think we could tell them what happened? And even if we agreed to tell them, do they really want to know? They're not going to challenge him. His father isn't going to take him out the back and beat him 'til he tells the truth, Father. That's never going to happen. Even if he did admit it, they'd find a way of blaming Antoinette for teasing him, making him do it. You know well Father, his mother will defend him to the hilt."

Of course, Tomás was right.

"And, there were other factors, Father."

"What other factors?"

"Us. Them." Tomás replied and explained, "The Daltons hold all the cards. It's their son. They will protect him, and they have the Guards on their side. John Holton is in business with the Daltons, and Hubert Tyrrell as well. And, of course, the locals will take their side against us Keanes who are blow-ins and migrants. Believe me, Father, the locals, will stick together. They won't have any sympathy for us."

"But the Gardaí should know," the priest said. But he knew it was a feeble demand he was making. Antoinette was in the same predicament as poor Moya. Who would believe her? It was his word against hers.

The priest felt the anger of this man, and his family. And shared that anger. He was heartbroken for them and especially for Antoinette. He couldn't forget the look on her face as she told him what had happened. He remembered sitting beside her, not being able to look at that simple, innocent face. He had to look away. He looked instead at the statue of Our Lady on Antoinette's May Altar, appealed to it, asked Her for guidance. But it looked back at him, at them, in silence, the silent suffering of a Mother for Her son, and for Her children.

Chapter 25

The parish priest asked Father O'Byrne to sit down. They were in Father Caffrey's living room. The aroma of piped tobacco filled the room. It was the same brand his own father used. St Bruno plug tobacco. Newspapers were folded on the coffee table and the parish priest's Breviary sat on top.

"Well, Dan, I want you to know that I had a word with my niece."

"Oh, yes."

"I told her she had to marry that man or stop seeing him."

Father O'Byrne nodded, acknowledging what he heard. Then said, "She realises that if she decides to marry, she will lose her position."

"Yes, Dan, she knows that, but she's willing to make that sacrifice."

"Oh, so she's decided to, er, retire?"

Father Caffrey pulled out his pipe and was filling it, "Yes, sure Jamesie Roche is a big farmer. She won't be needing her job anymore."

"And what of the daughter, Moya?"

"Well, obviously we can't have her in the house under the circumstances."

"Yes, quite."

"And my niece, will, er, do her duty, as his wife."

"But you can't allow Moya…"

Father O'Byrne wasn't sure what he was going to say, or what he meant to say. But Father Caffrey was probably right. If Miss O'Malley was to be Mrs Roche, then having Moya around would…what? Not be necessary? What was he saying? His mind was in confusion. Was having a wife a protection for the daughter? Was having the daughter in the house a temptation for the husband? Was that why it would be necessary to get Moya out of the house?

He watched the parish priest sit back in his sofa smoking his pipe, the smoke rising like incense, the aroma scenting the room.

He sat back in imitation, rubbing his knees with his clammy hands, considering the situation. And why would Louise O'Malley agree to such an arrangement? Did she feel that it would be better for the daughter to be out of the house, now that she, as wife, occupied his bed? Was she okay with the arrangement? Then he thought, well, why wouldn't she be? After all, she could be agreeing in order to maintain her respectability. Better to be Mrs Roche, than a principal of a school who was living in sin with an unmarried man, who was abusing his daughter and who was now, conveniently, out of the house.

Father O'Byrne could see the devious logic of it, but while he felt discomfort, he could not fathom the reasons for his discomfort and, what else, distaste?

It was all distasteful, yet this was the way it had to be. Father Caffrey was right. Moya would have to leave for her own sake and for his niece's sake.

"Where would she go?" Father O'Byrne asked, finally.

"I know a convent in Dublin who will take good care of her."

"A convent?"

"Yes, she will be well taken care of. She'll spend some time there and, in due course, she can leave and she'll be able to do what she likes. Get a job, all that."

Father O'Byrne did not want to think too much about what he heard. It was too difficult to take in; there were too many blank spaces. What particular convent? What will she be doing there? He presumed she would be educated. That would be a good thing. He deferred to his superior who seemed to know what he was about. It might be the best thing, after all, for Moya. It wasn't safe for her to be in the same house as her father. She probably was better off in a convent where she would be safe. As for Miss O'Malley, soon to be Mrs Roche, well, she seemed happy with the situation. But why? Why would she agree to this arrangement? Did she think that he, Roche, would be satisfied, and that it was her duty, or function to satisfy him? Save him? She still didn't believe Moya, that must be it. Then he realised what was happening. It was the only way she could justify her marrying Roche. How could she, an intelligent woman, fall for a monster? It was preposterous. Moya had to be lying.

He shook his head. There was a bewilderment that life threw at you, what were you to do with it?

"Don't worry, Father, there are ways of dealing with issues and problems like this. It's unfortunate that these things have to be done, but we, as priests of our parishes, have a duty to our people. There are things they don't have to face, and, indeed, they expect us to take care of them. We do these things for our people."

Father O'Byrne wanted to believe that his parish priest was right, indeed, he probably was right, after all he was a man of experience, and he, Father O'Byrne, would more than likely come across similar 'difficulties' in the future and, he too, would be obliged to take care of them in his time as parish priest.

Should he mention Frankie Dalton and what he did to Antoinette? He was too weary. Another time. And even if he did tell Father Caffrey, what difference would it make? There was nothing either man could do. But he had a duty to report it to his superior, which he would, but not just now. Next week will be fine. He couldn't bring himself to talk about it.

"Don't worry about these things, Dan," Father Caffrey said as he stood to indicate that the meeting had ended, "the good nuns will take good care of her."

Chapter 26

It was Saturday night, Confession night. Father O'Byrne looked at his watch. It was late. The last person to come to confession was Mrs Fennessy, who had listed off her usual sins: lying to her husband about having less money than what she really had tucked away; her anger at her eldest daughter who 'wouldn't do a rap around the place', and she missed Mass last Sunday because she was 'dying with the head cold and sneezing real bad'. She didn't want to be 'annoying the people around her and giving them the flu'. He gave her his usual three Hail Marys and a Glory be and absolved her of her sins.

He was about to take off his Stole and make his way back to the Parish House for his supper, when he heard a movement.

"Bless me Father for I have sinned, it's three months since my last confession."

He recognised the voice. It was Tomás Keane, and indeed it was three months because Tomás only ever came to confession to fulfil his Easter Duties. So, why did he come now?

Father O'Byrne blessed him, "*In nomine Patris, et Fillii, et Spiritus Sancti*.... Well, my son what are your sins?"

"I am going to kill Frankie Dalton."

The priest was shocked into silence, not sure he heard correctly.

"What did you say?"

"I am going to murder Frankie Dalton."

Father O'Byrne rubbed his forehead, "Did you say you wanted to or going to? There's a difference, my son."

"I'm going to, Father."

What was he to do? He knew that this was no bluff. He recalled their last conversation in the car outside the Keane farm. The anger was too palpable to be easily forgotten or appeased. He recalled his own anger. Felt it as strongly as Tomás.

"Look, Tomás, I can understand your anger. But you can't do this."

"I need to do it, and I want your blessing to do it."

"I can't give you my blessing."

"Not you, Father, the Church's."

"What do you mean? The Church can't bless murder, Tomás."

Was this really happening, was he actually hearing a confession or was it a nightmare he was having? He rubbed the tightness out of his forehead, making sure he felt pain, so he knew it was real.

"Antoinette isn't improving, Father. She's getting worse. The reason is that that bastard will be back for the summer holidays and she's terrified he's going to attack her again."

"But, Tomás, for God sakes, it's murder you are talking about. You are breaking the law of God."

"What about justice, Father?"

"The law will take care of that."

199

"You mean the law of the land? But it won't, because you and me have already talked about this. You know as well as I do that nothing is going to be done."

The priest felt a nauseous dry pain in his stomach, he could hardly breathe. What was he to say to him?

"Let God deal with this, Tomás."

"He will deal with it. Through you and the Church."

"I don't understand what you are saying."

"God's justice, Father. You represent God's justice here on earth. The only way God is going to mete out justice is if we carry it out on His behalf."

"That's not the way God works."

"But you will be working for Him, you'll be doing it on His behalf."

"I'll be doing nothing of the sort, Tomás. Don't drag me into this."

"I'm not asking you to do it, Father, all I'm asking is that you bless it."

"This is absurd."

"Think of Antoinette, she deserves a good life, a happy life. She's living in terror, utter terror of seeing him again. He deserves to die for what he has done to her."

The priest continued rubbing his head, nodding, there was truth in what he was saying.

"Is it God's justice that she should suffer, and he get away with his evil? And he will only keep doing it, Father. He won't stop."

He was right. It would not stop with Antoinette. He, too, felt the anger, the frustration of nothing being done. But still, he, as a priest, could not condone such an action.

"But think of his parents. The loss to them."

"And what about Antoinette's parents, what about us. His parents don't deserve him. They never did anything for him only allowed him to do what he wanted and get away with it. You know that as well as I do."

"I know you're angry, but you have to allow God to punish. Only God can punish."

"But what about the law? If they knew what he did what would they do? What happens to abusers and murderers, Father, tell me that? They're jailed or hanged. Does God come down and tell the courts and the judges not to jail, not to hang? No. He is on their side. He's on the side of the law. He knows that evil people have to die, have to be jailed for the sake of society, to protect society and innocent children. The only difference is that we are not going to any court or look for any judge."

"You mean we become judge and jury?"

"Yes."

"You can't do that, Tomás."

"Why not? God is on our side; the only difference is that the state doesn't get involved. And why not, Father? The only reason why the courts don't do anything is because no one tells them the truth. Because they don't hear about it, because the people are afraid to take on the likes of Dalton and Holton, and the gossips in the village."

Father O'Byrne nodded. What he was saying made sense.

"It's me and you now, Father."

"Me?"

"Not you. You as the Church. The representative of the Church."

"I am not going to be party to a murder."

"It's not you. You don't get what I'm saying, Father. It's God, through you."

"Look, Tomás, I can't absolve you from this."

"I know you can't absolve me, Father. Only God can, and He will."

There was a noisy, clumsy, shuffle in the confessional box, and then silence. He could hear Tomás' feet echo in the building as he left.

Father O'Byrne sat in the dark silence. He was shaking. His mind was in turmoil. He could feel Tomás' anger and if he weren't a priest, he too, if he were a father, would feel the same. But to murder someone? He thought of Antoinette afraid to leave the house because that bastard was hanging around and would be for the whole summer. Who else would he attack? Another child from Miss Connaughton's class, now Miss Riordan's? He was capable of doing it again. If he did it once, he'll do it again, and again. When would it stop?

Anne's face came to mind. The same face he saw in the visitor's room in the parish house. The one who was torn with anguish and suffering for Moya and would for Antoinette as well if she knew about it. What would she do? Would she agree with the Keanes? Seek revenge? But was it revenge, really? Or was it, as Tomás said, justice?

He should die, he was sure she would say. It could have happened to her when she was child. Who knew? He was realising that children, especially girls, and women, were particularly vulnerable to men without conscience or humanity.

Why did Anne leave Garrydangan? And so suddenly? Then it dawned on him, and he was annoyed with himself for not realising. She was pregnant. She must have been. Was that why she looked so tired and worn out? He felt his stomach knotting in anger and anxiety. It was Tyrrell who let her down, wouldn't go after her and marry her. Protestants. They had no morals. They prey on our Catholic women use them and then throw them away.

What would he do to Hubert Tyrrell if he saw him walking down Garrydangan?

Call him out for a duel? He shook his head with exhaustion. Lunacy.

All this was too much.

You ask too much, Oh Lord. Too much.

Chapter 27

Three days later Tim Dooley knocked on the door of the priest's house. It was late. Father O'Byrne answered it himself because Mrs Daly had gone home.

"Come in, Tim. Is there something wrong?"

"No, Father, it's okay. I came with a message from Tomás. He wants you to meet him."

"Is something the matter with Antoinette?"

"He says you are to meet him at the Old Mill."

"What?"

"He says you have to walk. Not go by car. Just yourself."

"Why?"

But Tim didn't answer, he turned around and walked back in the direction of the post office where he and his sister lived.

It was a chilly night. He went inside to put on his walking shoes and overcoat. He walked past the post office and made his way to the bridge and turned left along the Droode River. Despite the darkness, he could make out the path as it meandered by the river. The clouds hung low and ominous. The Old Mill stood about a quarter of a mile down the river pathway. When he saw it in the gloomy night it reminded him of something from Dickens or Conan-Doyle. He saw an opening which was darker than the stone walls of the building.

There was a figure there. He recognised Michael Keane. Michael beckoned to him to follow him.

"Mind the stairs, Father," he said as he carefully climbed up into the dark narrow passageway which led to the stairs.

It was a difficult climb and he was out of breath when he found himself standing on what was once the upper loft.

He saw two figures standing by someone lying on the ground who was writhing and making muffled grunting noises. When he had adjusted his eyes, he realised it was Tomás Keane and Tim Dooley standing at the old factory window over the bound and gagged figure of Frankie Dalton.

"Thanks for coming, Father." Tomás greeted, "I think you know what this is about."

"Tim, what are you doing here?"

Tim didn't answer. He merely looked down on Frankie Dalton with deep contempt. Father O'Byrne knew there was no need to say more.

"We've asked you, Father, to come here to give him the Last Rites."

"You can't do this," he was addressing the three men. "This is murder."

"No, Father, it's God's justice." Tomás spoke for them. These men had planned this and were now executing it.

"What are you saying?"

"Frankie here, is so overwrought with guilt for what he has done," Tomás said, as he kicked Frankie in the stomach, "he has come up here to commit suicide. Isn't that right?" He addressed the shackled figure on the ground, gave him another kick. Frankie struggled to get free, but he couldn't move.

Father O'Byrne could see clearer now. Frankie was bound with a rope around his middle, both arms bound to this body, and his legs were tied. He was blindfolded and his mouth was gagged with similar cloth, and around his neck was a rope.

"This is wrong." The priest appealed to the men, "You can't do this."

"Too, late, Father. He has already been condemned."

"By whom?"

"His own actions."

"But you can't. You have no right."

"Yes, we have."

"Who gave you that right?"

"Our innocent child, Father," Tomás replied.

"We have to do this, Father," Tim Dooley spoke quietly and deliberately, "no one is going to punish him for what he did to an innocent child. We are doing this for her, because she can't do it herself."

"Are you going to hear his last confession and give him the Last Rites," Tomás said quietly, "or are you not? One way or the other, Father, Frankie Dalton is going to meet his Maker tonight. Now, he can die in sin, or he can die absolved; he can die with the benefits of the sacraments, or he can't. It's up to you, Father," he looked down at the bound body, "and him."

The priest approached the prone body and knelt down beside him. Frankie was grunting trying to say something.

"Can't you at least allow him to speak?"

Tomás reached down and pulled out the cloth covering his mouth.

"You fucking bastards," Frankie shouted, "I'll get you for this."

"Shut up you bollix," Michael kicked him in the stomach, "listen to what Father O'Byrne has to say to you."

The priest blessed himself and made the sign of the cross over Frankie, "Let me hear your confession."

Frankie Dalton kicked about, but couldn't connect, "You can all just fuck off with yourselves."

"Are you not going to make a last confession?" Tomás was leaning over him now, pulling the rope around his neck, choking him, "Confess what you did to my daughter, you bastard."

Frankie turned in the direction of the voice, "Fuck off," and he spat at him.

"That's it," he nodded to Tim Dooley and his son, Michael. "Back away, Father."

As if it had been rehearsed, the priest watched as the three men stood him up and with quick movements cut the rope around his ankles and waist, ripped off the blindfold; all the while Frankie struggled to break free, but the three men moved swiftly and in unison, not giving him a chance to take any advantage over them; Michael grasped his legs, Tomás his arms and shoulders, Tim Dooley lifted his back, they set his body on the window ledge and in the blink of an eye hurled him over the edge. Frankie Dalton disappeared into the darkness.

Father O'Byrne heard a snap and then a cracking of bone. He ran to the window and looked down. Frankie Dalton was dangling from the rope. He saw the last convulsions of a body fighting to stay alive, arms flailing about and then Frankie Dalton's hands dangling by his side and his neck was contorted in a painful angle.

And then there was silence.

Father O'Byrne stood at the window. He couldn't look at the dead body any longer. He said a prayer for Frankie

Dalton's soul, and hoped that God would forgive him for the evil he had done in his life; and he said a prayer for himself, asking for forgiveness for not being able to stop what had just taken place.

He heard the shuffling of feet behind him. Tomás was saying to Michael to make sure they had everything. Tim Dooley came over to him and handed him a folded piece of paper, and then walked away, following the others down the stairs.

It was an envelope. There was a stamp and an address on it he couldn't make out because of the darkness. He put it in his overcoat pocket and walked back alone to the priest's house.

When he walked in the door, he put on his living room light and took out the envelope.

It was addressed to Tim Dooley. He opened the envelope. There was another envelope inside, addressed to him, Father Daniel O'Byrne, Garrydangan.

He took the letter out and read. It was from Doreen Heneghan. She wrote that Anne was staying with her in Birmingham, had a job as a seamstress in the same place she was working.

The next paragraph shocked and stunned him so much he fell into the chair, he could hardly breathe. It said that the reason why Anne had to leave Garrydangan was because she was raped by Frankie Dalton and that she was pregnant.

The following morning Garda John Holton came to the priest's house requesting that Father O'Byrne accompany him to the Old Mill. That there was a dead body that he ought to attend to. Father O'Byrne was in a panic. Would the Guard be asking questions? Where was he last night? Did he know anything about what happened?

Garda Holton drove the police car down the lane to the Mill. Tim Dooley was standing over the dead body of Frankie Dalton. He was spread-eagled on the ground. As they approached Father O'Byrne saw no sign of the rope.

"Tim here, found the body as he was taking his morning walk," Guard Holton explained to the priest. He looked up at the top of the old building. "He must have fallen. It's not safe up there. A stone or a rock gave way, I'd say."

Tim asked the priest to bless the dead body and say a few prayers for the repose of his soul. The three men stood over the body. Father O'Byrne prayed the last rites.

"Would you mind, Father, if yourself and Tim stay here until I get the undertaker to come and take the body to Clochdroode?"

Both men agreed readily.

"And if you don't mind, Father, I would appreciate you accompanying me to his family to give them the bad news."

Father O'Byrne said that of course he would.

John Holton made his way back to the car and returned to the Garda Station to make the necessary phone calls.

"What happened?" Father O'Byrne asked Tim, "last night he was hanging from a rope."

"Don't worry, Father. We took care of it."

Tim explained that the three men returned as soon as the priest went back to the parish house. They hauled his body back up, untied the rope from Dalton's neck and from that height let him fall down onto the stony ground below, and then left him lying there overnight. As far as Holton was concerned Tim came as usual for his morning walk and discovered the body.

"But there'll be an inquiry, Tim. What'll we do then?"

"I'll tell them the truth. I discovered the body about an hour ago. I walked back to the Garda station. Told John Holton what I saw. They will draw their own conclusions."

"What conclusion, Tim?"

"That he must have come last evening to climb the Mill. He was like that. A bit of an adventurer. Climbed to the top. He must have slipped, fallen and broke his neck."

"But there will be marks on his neck."

"He broke his neck in the fall. There will be bruises, obviously. John will have a word with the coroner. He will be told that Frankie was a troubled child. We don't want it to be seen as a suicide. We know what the Church says about suicide. He won't get a proper burial. We can't do that to the family, now can we?"

And so it transpired.

There was an inquiry. The coroner ruled death by misadventure. Frank Dalton's neck was broken in the fall. It was known to the people in Garrydangan that he was a bit of a wild one; it was not out of character for him to be taking all sorts of risks. Everyone knew how it was unsafe to be climbing to the top of the Old Mill. Sure, didn't they warn their children not to be climbing the derelict building.

It became the truth of what happened to Frankie Dalton, son of Frank Senior and Margaret Dalton.

Epilogue

"Father O'Byrne?" Stanley Payten addressed the old man as he entered the sacristy.

"And who are you?" the priest said gruffly, turning his bent back to him.

"Stanley Payten."

"Who?" The priest turned to take another look at the visitor, "never heard of you."

"You know my mother."

"What? What are you saying?"

"She's from, or was from, Garrydangan."

"How the hell would I know your mother?"

"Her name was Anne. Anne Connaughton."

Father O'Byrne slumped onto the floor. He was on his knees, his head sunk into his exhausted body, "Oh, God." His voice raspy and pained, "No."

Stanley went over to him and asked did he need help. The priest pointed to the chair. Stanley pulled the chair closer to the old man. He helped the priest to steady himself onto it.

"Why are you here?" the priest stared at the visitor.

"My mother, step-mother, mentioned your name whenever she spoke of Garrydangan."

"Your step-mother?"

"Doreen Heneghan was my step-mother. But I always called her 'my mother'. She was from around here."

"And your real mother was Anne Connaughton."

"Yes."

"Oh God," the priest mumbled to himself. Hearing her name again was a stab in his heart. He found it difficult to breathe. He tried to remember the face from so many years past. How many? Thirty? More?

"Are you okay, Father?" Stanley asked. "Can I get you a drink of water or something?"

Father O'Byrne waved him away. There was another seat. He pointed to it.

Stanley sat on it. "I'm here to do some research, Father."

"Research?"

"I'm researching for an article on the Pope's visit to Ireland. And while I was here, I decided to visit my mother's home place."

"I see." Father O'Byrne was holding his chest. There was a particular pain there he hadn't felt for a long time. He now had a picture of her in his mind. His head slumped to his chest, "Oh, Anne," he whispered.

Stanley didn't hear what the priest said, assumed it was a prayer of some kind. "What was she like? My mother, my real mother, Anne Connaughton?"

Father O'Byrne looked at his visitor more closely. He had her eyes, green-flecked, and her skin. He wasn't like Doreen, who was fair-skinned and freckled.

The priest managed a feeble smile, "You look like her."

"That's what Doreen always said." Stanley smiled, pleased with what he heard, "But what was she like, what kind of person was she? I hope you don't mind me asking you all these questions."

Father O'Byrne shook his head, saying nothing. What was there to say?

"She was a very good person," he had to say something to this man, this son of Anne Connaughton, "a lovely person. Her children, her pupils, loved her." He felt a clutch at his heart remembering her.

"If you don't mind me asking, what happened to her?"

"What do you mean?" He had to be careful. He played for time to gather his thoughts. "I'm sure you know more about her than I would. What did Doreen tell you?"

"Only that she taught here and had to leave her job because she was pregnant with me. That in those days it was a scandal for an unmarried woman, especially a teacher, to have a baby."

"That's correct." The priest's hands were clammy; the uncertainty of what this young man, the son of Anne Connaughton, knew, or did not know, intensified. "Unfortunately, that was the law at the time." But he had questions of his own to ask. "What happened to her when she went to England?"

Stanley's eyes became pained with sad memories. "She died soon after having me. Doreen said it was a difficult birth. Anne, my mother, wasn't well at the time. I don't know what was wrong, but she found the birth difficult."

The priest continued to stare at the young man. He didn't want to know any more. He had had enough information. Poor, beautiful Anne. God be good to her, my lovely Anne.

"Doreen and Tommy Payten her husband raised me." Stanley went on with his story, "They had no children themselves. Tommy Payten was an army man who fought in the war, returned home with some kind of mental trouble, depression or something, and ended up in a military hospital and died soon after I was born. So, I was pretty much brought up by Doreen."

"And Doreen? How is she?"

"She died a few years ago."

"I'm sorry, I never knew what happened to her and Anne after they left. I never heard."

"It was hard. I miss her. She was a wonderful person, kind and always smiling. Positive, you know. Not like me."

"What did you do?"

"Me?" Stanley dismissed his importance, "Oh, I went to the local Grammar. Did a degree in Birmingham University. English and Politics. Did a little work for the Labour Party, local MP Ted Noone. Gave that up. Got a little disenchanted with the whole politics game. Ended up in journalism. You know, bits and pieces, here and there."

"Very good, very good." Father O'Byrne was feeling more confident now. He told him how great it was to see Anne's son, and wished him well in his research. He was about to say, it was nice meeting you, and goodbye.

"I was wondering, Father, if you could help me with something."

"Oh, what is that?" The priest grew anxious. He feared that this young man was on a trail seeking information that he could not and would not tell.

"I was going through my mother's papers. Doreen's, I mean. I mean stuff she had, bits and pieces, you know."

"Yes." The priest held his breath.

"I came across a letter, a letter written by a Tim Dooley."

Oh, God, please, no. Don't put me through this.

"Oh, yes, of course, Tim. Tim was the sacristan in Garrydangan for many years. He was in bad health and died about ten years ago. Poor man. Never took care of himself. Heavy smoker."

The priest struggled to maintain calm, hoped his nervousness wasn't showing. He felt a cold flush down his back.

"It's the only thing I have from anyone from Garrydangan. It's my only real link, besides Doreen herself. I wished I had seen it before she died." Stanley took an envelope out of his pocket and took out a letter. "It's very short. It's really only one line." He unfolded it and read from it, "It's addressed from the Post Office, Garrydangan."

No, Lord. Don't do this, I can't take any more.

"That would be right. Tim's sister was the post-mistress. He lived with his sister most of his life."

"I was wondering about that. He addressed her and asks how my mother is. That would be Anne. Then he writes this, which is all there is to the letter, really. He says that 'Dalton got his come-uppance'. That's it. Dalton got his come-uppance. He signs it off with 'Yours sincerely, Tim'. Who is this Dalton person? Was he from around here?"

A shot of relief went through the priest's body.

"You mean, Doreen never mentioned this to you. This Dalton person?"

"No. And I have been trying to find out, and nobody seems to know. I phoned the Post Office in Garrydangan. This was after I discovered the letter. Whoever answered the phone said that she did not know any Daltons, that as far as she could tell there was no family of that name in Garrydangan. She said, why didn't I try Clochdroode. But nobody knew anything there either."

Father O'Byrne relaxed and thought for a moment. He had to be careful, he could still feel the cold sweat trickle down his back.

"The Dalton's got their come-uppance? Is that what Tim said?"

"Yes."

"Well, all I can think of is that she is referring to Frank Dalton who owned some businesses in Garrydangan years back." He felt a little more confident as he spoke, "The Daltons thought they were big-shots in the village; he and his wife thought they were above the rest of the people. Always had to be one-up on everyone. Had big plans to set up a quarry business. But it went bust."

"What happened?"

"Doreen's father had to sell the farm because of health reasons, as you probably know. Well, it caused some trouble here."

"Why would it?"

"Well, there were people in the village felt that someone who should have gotten a chance to buy the Heneghan farm never got an opportunity to put in a bid."

"Who were they?"

"The Keanes."

"She never mentioned them. The Keanes? No. Who were they?"

"Neighbours of the Heneghans. They had the farm next to theirs. But they never got the farm. The Daltons that Tim Dooley mentioned and a few of his buddies, set up a kind of consortium to open a gravel pit. You know the quarry nearby?

You drove past it on your way here. It's part of the Esker Rí. It runs from here down to Garrydangan. Well, the feeling would have been that Dalton deprived the Keanes of the Heneghan farm. It would have been perfect for the Keanes."

"What happened to them, I mean the Keanes?"

"They had their troubles, as a result. Their farm wasn't big enough to make a living. Michael the oldest had to leave for England. Ended up on the buildings in London. The younger lad got married and did the best he could, but eventually, he sold it off after the parents died. But that was later. The 'come-uppance' that Tim is talking about was probably because Dalton never held up his side of the bargain. He cheated on his business partners. He bought the Heneghan farm but he never paid for it."

"Why not?"

"He was relying too much on his wife's money. Money which she never had because her brother disputed her father's will."

"This is very complicated and confusing."

"Well, the story is all too familiar, here in Ireland, where families are in dispute with one another over land or property. Basically, Dalton counted his chickens before they were hatched. He owed for the farm, but his partners had to cough up. Leaving him with a bill to pay. I suppose that's what Tim Dooley meant when he said that he got his come-uppance. He probably thought, like many in Garrydangan, that he lied his way into buying a farm he could not afford and thereby denied a local man the farm. The Heneghans would have wanted the Keanes to have the farm, but Dalton outbid them, over-extended himself, relying on his wife's money which never materialised, and he was punished."

"What happened to him?"

By now, Father O'Byrne had his narrative in place. "Tragic really. The Daltons had a son who died under tragic circumstances. They never recovered. They sold the business and moved to a house outside Clochdroode."

"How did he die?"

The narrative would contain lies, but also truth.

"Ah, sure, poor lad, he was climbing the Old Mill, which was unsafe. Fell. Killed."

Stanley refolded the letter and put it back in the envelope. "That was always a mystery to me. Glad it's now cleared up. So, this Tim Dooley was basically telling my mother that their farm went to the wrong person; that their neighbours should have got it, didn't, and the Daltons were punished for their greed. Is that it?"

"That would be about it, alright."

But the priest was becoming agitated again. Too many memories were flooding through him. He had spent years trying to forget the past, years trying to deny it. Why did this person, who looked so like her, come back? Was God punishing him? Yes, He was. His heart wasn't strong. How would it bear up to all these terrible and awful memories?

"Do you know who my father was?"

The priest managed to shake his head as if to recall the deep and distant and long forgotten past.

"What did Doreen tell you?"

"She said he was an army man like my dad, her husband, Tommy Payten. But I never believed it."

"Why not?" His stomach creaked with fear. It was all going to come out. He's pretending. He knows more than he says.

Stanley bowed his head and rested it in his hands and put the weight of it on his knees. He didn't speak. He rubbed his eyes and kept rubbing them until he lifted his head and looked away from the priest.

Father O'Byrne sat in total fear that this young man knew everything. The anxiety that was inside him hadn't left, not since the moment he heard Anne Connaughton's name. He sat opposite a man in deep distress. He didn't ask him was he okay. He didn't want to speak to him anymore. He wanted to tell him to leave. That he had seen enough of him, that he reminded him too much of his mother, that it was too sad. That he and the Church were stupid, that he should have told Anne that she could stay, she could marry a Protestant, that it didn't matter. She could hold onto her job, stay in Garrydangan. She could have his child. But it wasn't Hubert's child. He wished it were. It would have been so much easier. But instead... He didn't want to think about that.

"Why would you not believe Doreen? I can tell you that she, Anne, did go out with an army man."

"She did? Who?"

"A Captain Hubert Tyrell. Have you ever heard of him?"

"No, she never mentioned him."

"Then you must try and find him." A strange relief came over the priest, at last he could help this young man, and at the same time get rid of him. "Do some research, I'm sure you'll track him down. Tyrrell of Tyrrell House, Garrydangan. I'm sure you'll find archives somewhere."

But all the while the priest was thinking, why didn't Doreen tell him? Surely she knew of their relationship? She above any other would have known about it. Why not tell Anne's son of, at least, the possibility? Why not? It would have been a way to avoid the truth. He remembered the night, that same night, when Tim Dooley handed him the letter. Then it was true. He hadn't wanted to believe Tim. That it was him. He raped Anne. He was the father.

Oh, my God. How much pain must we endure?

Oh, God, You have made us and we have turned against You. We have become evil and destruction in the world. We are the bringers of darkness and all the Darknesses that ever was and ever shall be!

The priest looked at the young man sitting in front of him, his head in his hands. He is her son, but also his. He recognised it in him.

"Yes, I will. I will do some more research."

"Good," the priest was relieved, at last he could now bid this man a goodbye.

"But it doesn't really matter, Father."

"Why? I thought you wanted to find out about your parents."

"I do, of course I do. I'm writing about Ireland and Irish Catholicism, as I told you. But the article on the Pope's visit, I realise, now is only a prop to explore something deeper. It's my opportunity to find out things about myself, my past, where I'm really from. You know?"

"Yes," Father O'Byrne agreed, "of course."

"But when I drove up here and attended your Mass this morning, I realised something. I am at home here. I looked at the congregation and felt that this is where I belong, or came from. It doesn't matter about who my father was, what matters is who I am now, what I am."

"What you say makes sense, Stanley. At the end of the day, all that matters is who we are now. Our parents don't matter, or they do, but not essential to who you are, as an individual, as a child of God."

"I'm not a religious person, Father so, I'm not sure where God comes in. Okay, I think I get your meaning. But there are things about myself I have to deal with, and it doesn't matter who my mother was, or who my father was."

The priest did not say anything; he could only listen.

"There's one thing that bothers me, Father. I'm not sure why I am saying this or telling you this." He looked up and saw a pain and a suffering in the old priest that he thought might help him. This priest knew something about life and its hardships, he sensed. He would know its cruelties and disappointments. He would understand.

"It's something that has been bothering me for a long time, Father. I don't know why I bring it up now. Maybe it's because you are a priest. You are my connection to my family and my past. Maybe I feel I can talk to you."

Father O'Byrne waited. This was a troubled soul, and as a priest he had a duty to listen and give comfort where he could.

"I've never been able to hold onto a relationship, Father. I don't know what's wrong with me. I have these thoughts. Frightful thoughts at times. I can get angry. I find it difficult to cope with the disappointment of rejection, and not being able to get on with women. It's as if the women I want to be with eventually realise they don't want to be with me. And I say things and do things which only makes things worse."

Stanley watched for the priest's reaction. He was listening with patience and understanding.

"I'm kind of making a kind of confession here, Father. I mean I'm in the right place for it, right? Well, I'm in my thirties, Father. I feel I should have found someone by now. But sometimes I get down. I get depressed. I think my life won't work out." He put his head in his hands, "I'm sorry, Father. This is not really a confession or anything. I'm not even a practising Catholic."

Father O'Byrne felt sorry for him. He knew what he was feeling. And he had an idea where it came from, or from whom it originated. Captain Hubert Tyrrell was not Stanley's father, but he should have been, not him. His heart ached for Stanley and for Anne. What kind of life did she have when she left? What pain and hardship, loneliness and isolation? Thanks be to God for Doreen. He hoped this young man would take after the women in his life. But it seemed like it wasn't going to be like that. There was nothing he could do for this young man. He was born in sin, a sin not his, and he suffers for it. We all have suffered for it.

The priest stood feebly on his feet. He was tired; this meeting had gone on for too long. He had to get back to the house. He had to send this man on his way. There was no use in telling this young man the truth. The truth would do nothing for him.

"I hope I was of help, Mr Payten."

Stanley raised himself stiffly from the chair.

"Thanks, Father, you've been a great help."

They shook hands.

The priest showed him out of the sacristy and walked him through the small Church. Outside the sun was struggling to burn through the grey sky. Father O'Byrne watched him get in his red Datsun and drive away.

Father Daniel O'Byrne walked slowly and painfully back to the priest's house which was only a hundred yards from St Fiacha's Church. The house smelled of must and damp. But he never noticed, and when he did, he accepted it as his lot. He didn't have a housekeeper. He didn't need one. He cooked for himself and took care of himself.

He made his way upstairs and went into his bedroom. There was a single bed in the corner with sheets that needed washing. He would change them sometime. Over the bed was a simple crucifix. There were no photographs on the walls or on the dressing table. It was a monastic cell. The only picture he permitted himself was a picture of the Sacred Heart with a red votive lamp plugged into the wall, and in the corner an Altar with a statue of Our Lady of the Immaculate Conception. There were no flowers.

He made his way to the wardrobe and opened it. He reached up and pulled out a leather trousers belt. He took off his shirt and knelt down on the wooden floor in front of the picture of the Sacred Heart. He bowed to it with a deep reverence and blessed himself and then wrapped the belt around his right hand until he it was tight and began whipping himself on his bare back.

He lashed himself crying out an appeal to God and the Blessed Mother to forgive him.

He kept whipping himself until the pain became bearable, and then he continued until he could no longer bear it.

He then stopped until the pain eased, all the while he prayed that his sins would be taken away.

"Lamb of God, Lamb of God, take away the sins of the world.

Lamb of God take away my sins, and the sins of the world."

Then he started again, lashing himself, and crying out.

"Oh Lord I am not worthy.

Oh Lord I am not worthy."

And he kept whipping himself until he could bear it again, and then continued until he was overcome with pain and became faint.

And it was always at this moment that he thought of them. Revenants excavated from memory. Anne, Antoinette and Moya. And he cried for them, tears of a deep anguish he could not fathom, and he prayed that these tears would never cease; and that he would never manage to fathom them, for if he did, he would come to understanding, and he did not deserve to understand and find peace in this understanding.

How could he find peace?

How did he deserve peace?

He had denied Anne her freedom; he had denied his love for her, a love that would have granted her what she desired, which was to marry Hubert Tyrrell, and he denied what he realised was what he would have wanted for himself. But it was too late.

He never found out what happened to Moya. She disappeared into a nether world of blankness.

The only memory he had of Antoinette was of her coffin being lowered into her grave in Garrydangan. She died too young and suffered so much it was a blessing God took her to Himself.

It was the same routine each night. He flagellated himself until he fainted and slumped onto the floor. And each time he came out of the faint, it was after midnight.

And each night was the same.

He prayed that God would show him mercy and allow him to remember Antoinette's sweet and innocent face; of that child he prayed with in her bedroom at the simple altar before she received her First Holy Communion.

But God refused to grant him his request.

All he could remember was her coffin being lowered into a grave, and it being filled with Esker clay.

It was God's punishment. For what he did and what he should have done.

"Oh Lord, I am not worthy.

Oh Lord, I am not worthy."

He raised himself up and knelt on the hard floor and looked into the eyes of the Sacred Heart.

And to his horror each time he looked, he looked into the eyes of Frankie Dalton.